For
A Cacamander

TANUJA MULLICK

ISBN 978-93-52011-64-3

First published in India 2019 by Inkstate Books
An imprint of Leadstart Publishing Pvt Ltd

Sales Office:
Unit No.25/26, Building No.A/1,
Near Wadala RTO,
Wadala (East), Mumbai – 400037 India
Phone: +91 9699933000
Email: info@leadstartcorp.com
www.leadstartcorp.com

Disclaimer: The Views expressed in this book are those of the Author and do not pertain to be held by the Publisher.

Editor: Abhishek Chandran
Cover: Victorpatali
Layouts: Victorpatali
illustration: Teyesha Mullick

Dedicated

To,

A few good men

(The best of whom are dead)

Contents

About the Author

Tanuja Mullick is a Post Graduate in Sociology with an AMI ((Association of Montessori International) Diploma. She has worked in a geriatric care home in Wales when her husband was in the University of Swansea, and taught very briefly at an international school in South Bombay. She has written two books previously, published by, Cyberwit. One book of poems and another on family and food.

Tanuja has lived in a few places and travelled a bit before and after marriage.

Her uncle Abraham Eraly and her husband Sumit Mullick inspired her to add to the book collection.

Her daughter Teyesha designed the book covers of the published works.

Acknowledgements

Thanking you,

My father who always had dreams for me,

My mother for giving me plenty of books in my childhood and later,

My husband for leading the book trail,

My daughter, for everything and yet another book cover design,

Musically evolved friends for their notes,

Google, omniscient and generous.

Strangers, friends and well-wishers,

Bookshelf, please do not fade into obscurity,

Memory, abide with me.

Gratefully yours,
Tanuja Mullick
2018

Glossary

Axis Of Action	-	Imaginary Line Where 24 Frames Are Shot per Second
Padmasan	-	Yoga Posture Of Lotus
Pahadi	-	Of The Hills (A Denizen)
Yaar	-	Friend Or Pal, Colloquial
Aiyee	-	Mother In Marathi
Yeh	-	This
Laadli Betis	-	Favourite Daughters
Mashaals	-	Fire Torch
Mali	-	Gardener
Mehraba	-	Hello, In Turkish
Mirch Ki Salan	-	Green Pepper Curry
Firnee	-	An Eastern Rice Pudding
Kamdeva Rati Sadhana	-	Yogic Rite, An Elixir
Saala	-	Brother In Law In Hindi, *Also An Abuse Word*
Saale	-	Plural Of Saala
Poda Maire	-	A Common Phrase Used By Malayalis, A Mild Abuse, "Pull Pubic

Hair"

Azaan	- Call To Prayer, Recited From Mosques
Mallu	- Malayali
Molay	- Affectionate Term For Daughter, In Malayalam
M. I.	- Medical Inspection
Wah!	- Wow!
Kya Baat Hai!	- That Is Great News!
Rishta	- Relationship
Rishvat	- Bribe
Sarkar	- Government
Jhubba	- Kurta For Men In Kerala
Mundu	- Male Sarong Worn In Kerala
Par	- But
Amar Prem	- Eternal Love
Bhabiji	- Brother's Wife, Also Term For Any Married Woman In N. India
Pett	- Stomach
Puja	- Worship
Gyan	- Knowledge
Bata Bati	- Distribution Or Sharing
Sant	- Saint
Dar	- Fear
Aap / Thum	- You

Hum	- We
Sab	- All
Raita	- A Curd Relish
Kaali peeli	- Black yellow (cabs)
Baingan	- Brinjal/Aubergine
Kaali peeli	- Black and yellow cabs
Ram	- Biblical reference (Ancestor of King David)
Badla	- Metal wire embroidery

1

Sliding Windows

Organic threads tied to the fringes of the great beyond give an illusion of an intricate pane. The quotidian lies between the folds of a scrim.

Out of the now, a sub-let apartment on the second floor of Duromer Place, a mechanical engineering student whose name sounded Indian was going home on vacation and was renting out his 'three and a half' for a month. A mother and daughter were the aspirants who hoped to be his temporary tenants. The girl was also a student in the same university and introduced her mother to the boy.

"My mum is visiting. She will now be here for less than four weeks. I share a condo near St. Lawrence with a white Anglophone couple." The prospective Landlord broke into a wide smile as empathy vacuumed the spotty parts.

"Do we need permission to live here?" asked

the older woman, the wife of a bureaucrat. The emphatic "Oh, no, not at all!" from the boy was reassuring.

"We are from India, I am Mrs Rai. Where are you from?"

"Very good! I am from Islamabad." Zamsher Khan said with a wry smile.

Antana, the daughter, quickly interjected, "My grandmother was also from there." The boy looked surprised.

"Lahore was where my mother in law was born, and her father was the Registrar of Lahore University," said the lady.

Zamsher, cheerfully declared, "I am international!"

The deal was sealed with more than half the rent paid in advance. The Indians, relieved and pleased they would be out of the Condo, walked back humming snatches of old favourite songs in English and Hindi. Antana wanted her mother to sing a Tamil song that their beloved *ayah* used to sing to the mother and daughter when they were both in infancy in their respective time lines.

Mrs Rai turned to her daughter, "Precious, had I known you would have to go through such lengths to organize my stay and that your flatmates were uncomfortable with my presence, I would have come for just a fortnight. Your father insisted I should stay for two months. Oof! Good thing I made it just seven weeks."

"Aww, ma! Don't take this personally. It's a cultural construct. Here they hardly mix with their own folks. They have no clue about parents and adult-kid bonding. It is difficult for them to have their folks around for more than a weekend. You are pushing off to America for a week to be out of their way. The day after you return we shall leave at the crack of dawn and take a day trip to Ottawa. We will return late and the next day, we pack and move to Duromer. Let's just make the most of time and space. I am so happy to have my mamma here with me." Antana reached out to link her arm with her mother and said, "The people out here seeing us will probably think we are a couple."

"Eesh, yuck! How sick, when one look at us and they will know I am your birth mother. Bah! My seven months of complete bed rest during pregnancy and thirty-four hours of labour pain should not be reduced by one glance from sacred to the disgustingly profane. Such sick people!"

At the beginning of the fresh new month, two rents were paid, one each to the condo mates and for the sub-let. Zamsher's flat mate Ali had asked them to pay up the balance of payment the day they moved into the flat, and Ali moved out.

Both the boys had neatly spruced up the flat. Wardrobes and dressing table drawers had been emptied and everything was shipshape in the airy and comfortable single bedroom. There was a single bed parallel to the large window. On the opposite side, along the length of the wall was a thick mattress. The kitchenette was a quarter in the 3 ½. A comfortable size sitting room was the main hall cum dining and kitchen. The bathroom was the third room. The sheer luxury of not having to share the bathroom with any outsider was most satisfying. Mrs Rai shuddered to think of poor Antana having to often run to the nearest Sam Morton's to use the facility because the Vancouver girl who was her flat-mate, a bog-hog, would have long conversations on her phone in the bathroom. The manager, after the first fortnight, told Antana that she would have to buy something first in order to use the facility. She told her daughter that if ever she could afford to buy her a place in Canada she would make sure that it would have at least an extra toilet and a bedroom with attached bathroom. Antana smiled indulgently.

Two new scented candles and a matchbox placed in the blue and grey tiled bathroom were thoughtful touches, thought Mrs Rai. She marvelled at the housekeeping, for everything was in its proper place. She wondered aloud if Indian boys would have been so meticulous. The fridge had been emptied. In Ali's hurry to clean up he had spilled some *biryani* in the freezer. She had to put the fridge off, for a while, to clean it up. She told Antana that pork products would have to be kept in separate boxes that did not belong to the boys and cooked in their own pans and pressure cooker with their own spoons and ladles. Respecting other religious beliefs and taboos was a principle ingrained in the mother as her father was a very generous and tolerant person.

Antana was a by product of an inter-state, inter-faith marriage. It was unconventionally conventional as her parents had had an arranged marriage. Mr and Mrs Rai decided to have her baptized when she was three months old, even though the father was officially a Hindu. The mother belonged to the ancient Christian sect known as the Syrian Orthodox Christians. But she had to become a member of the Church of South India of the Anglican denomination to get the baby baptized. In fact, she was doing a spot of research on the Orthodox Syrian Church in the university library while Antana was busy with her Master's degree thesis.

Windows in three layers in the hall cum kitchenette and in the bedroom opened out to the lush green of a pretty tree. Mrs Rai could not identify it but was almost sure that it was neither maple nor sycamore. Red brick building of various heights had turned their backs to them.

With deft little touches, Mrs Rai made their transit place a home. The ten storeyed 10 Duromer Place saw an assortment of students from Asia, particularly the South East. Young Caucasian men in sharp business suits, and East

European and Latin American men wilted past their salad days. Two old Chinese women cleaned the general areas. The part time managerial staff was also Chinese.

When the scrimped drapes darkened the white nights, it was a deep sleep. Dawn spread light early for they were East of the East. The city was also in the South East of the country. As Mrs Rai slid the windows open she saw a white man sitting on top of the low wooden stairway of the brick red triplex house. Attractive with muddy red-brown hair that, left to its natural state, would curl in pleasure. Scissors had trimmed and teased it to stand straighter. He sat there and smoked. Was he looking inward as he gazed out? Was he local, or American, or European? Did he speak English with a Quebecois accent? Mrs Rai's curiosity peaked. As she moved from the viewing point, she slid the mesh windows between the two glass ones into lock position. Later when she glanced out he was gone. A black car was parked in the back yard. She'd missed seeing it when she first spotted the cigarette smoking man. Smoke and cigarettes were a sore point in their home. Antana, at age six, was with her mother visiting someone when the old lady of that house recounted how a 35-year-old police officer they knew had dropped dead due to a cardiac arrest, and for good measure she added it was due to excessive smoking. Antana panicked as her father was a chain smoker. That night, she knelt before her bed and fervently prayed that her father stopped smoking. He never did. To the little girl, it meant that her prayer had not been answered, Perhaps there really was no higher authority to grant her wish. That was the beginning of her atheism.

The smoker only smoked outside his home. A man who chose to keep the home smoke and nicotine free was a decent man by her reckoning.

Back home, even the cemetery had more life than that street alley. Quiet and lifeless, a world set apart from her part of the world. Next to the smoker's barren patch was a green ivy veil designed to hide the wooden fence; with Molina grasses and cubes and rectangles that create a kind of evergreen maze. Vertical interest created by the acer palmatum was a perfect foil to counter the sturdy Maple on the other side. The interlocking triangles were filled with orange, yellow and pink liliums, red and pink geraniums and a bonsai conifer. A miniature Japanese style temple in concrete was slightly off centre to the right. Japanese anemones grew in respectful numbers. It resembled a far Eastern oasis. A big fan of lush lawns, Mrs Rai thought it would have given the little garden an arresting quality.

Twin houses with very different exteriors and probably totally different interiors too, reflected different cultures. A small Asian man was seen tending the garden with total devotion. The two men, the smoker and the garden owner were back to back but oblivious to each other. To an onlooker, it was eye candy. The two were so easy to gaze at, so hard to define.

The small wooden deck was evidently a smoking zone. The white man would sit and smoke, spit and smoke, sip and smoke, speak on the cell phone and smoke, read and smoke, text and smoke, or just stare and smoke. There was a lot of smoking. In Bombay, cigarette vendors had tiny stalls at street corners. Their observation was that of a gender divide. Their customer base was now more girls while the boys were falling short.

On the first Saturday morning of that month she saw the man, dapper in tennis shorts and T-shirt, load a wicker basket of laundry into the boot, drop a racquet on the back seat and speed off in his black BMW.

The mesh window slid open. The pretty green tree waved its leafy arms. She named it 'Anamika' which in Sanskrit meant nameless. A pleasantly cool breeze wafted into their bedroom. It was ironic that in Montreal in May of that year, Antana had walked miles to buy a pedestal fan for her room in the Condo. The boys had a small table fan in the bedroom. 'Anamika' was more right handed, Mrs Rai thought, as its left arm was stiffly still but symmetrically covered in foliage. Was it a Canadian version of the shisham tree, planted by the first Nation Fathers when this was their land? Their descendants were seen sprawled on street corners, wallowing in their liquor induced puke. In it lay quarks of exploitation and inequality. Their reality was to be scared away by lighting up potent weed or drowned in cheap liquor. In spiralling columns of smoke and pools of vomit they sniffed out possibilities and drowned sorrows.

An online news link carried an article on Antana's father. Antana was going through it and then suddenly turned to her mother saying, "It says papa is the third Dalit to take up this prestigious post. How funny! Don't they do their homework? Not that there's anything wrong with that in the slightest, but why would they call him a Dalit?" Mrs Rai stopped her window cleaning and came over to read the article. She clicked her tongue and said, "They can never give an accurate account. Here they say Calcutta-born and have reduced him to a March baby when he was born in April, Eliot's cruellest month! Your father was born in New Delhi." Mrs Rai went back to the window with her duster. She sensed the absence of the backyard men. Unknown to them, she had christened them both. BMW Baba was the White man and Blossoms Baba was the Oriental man. Antana laughed when her mother told her and said, "Smokie and Mali are spot on."

The view directly in front of the window was a puzzle. There were four types of facades and multi-entry points through a big wooden gate. Different apartments had been culled out of that. When mass migration from Europe into North Americas happened, the older settlers of generations gone by who were property owners became the ruling class. Not all of them thought that it was history playing over, they turned into savvy businessmen. They turned single family homes into smaller apartments from basement to attic. From simple to complex is the story of the 'plex' – a three to four level squat building block of different dimensional apartments. A metal or wooden stairway outside was constructed. Hazardous, slippery, icy stairways in sub-zero temperatures formed the thin ice on the skating rink of the immigration ballet. 'Objective illusion'' seemed apt in this case where desperate immigrants failed to see exploitation. Self-interest versus survival became the narrow confines of refugee classism. Cultures grow through conquest, immigration, intermingling, imitation and conversion. The external staircase became the architectural hallmark of the city. Multiculturalism, propelled by the flow of immigrants and economics, is successful with wide open spaces and where materialism is manifold.

Through the windows she painted mindscape portraits. BMW Baba was probably here on a business project while home was elsewhere. Spitting and flicking ash in your own backyard was not worthy of a homeowner. He even threw cigarette stubs around the compound. His work spot was apparently close enough for him to zip in and out. Often, his BMW was seen at different times of the day during the week. Very rarely was it seen at all during the weekend. Cigarette puffs and a hot beverage from a black mug marked these office breaks. Not once did Mrs Rai see him chew, munch or eat. Blossom Baba looked cheerless and woebegone. Did cultural lag weigh him down?

She asked her daughter Antana to wish Zamsher and Ali for Eid-ul-Fitr. Zamsher thanked her profusely from Islamabad, Ali, from some building in the vicinity. Back in Bombay, Mr Rai was probably enjoying mutton biryani, *mirch ki salan* and *firnee* that Mr Tripathi, a Brahmin, always sent. Mr Tripathi was a Good Samaritan who believed strongly in communal harmony, and the NGO he had set up was to educate Muslim children in the cow belt areas up North. He also did a lot to help butchers.

That morning Antana again read something about her father being a Scheduled Caste and she laughed perplexedly at the ludicrous statement. Her father's grandfather was a *rai bahadur,* a title no Scheduled Caste could have had. In fact, their surname was derived from the title given by the British to her great grandfather who had been a government official. Her father's father had been a Cambridge blue in tennis before he joined the Indian Civil Service. The old homestead back in Calcutta was the house bought by her grandfather's father and must have been impressive in days of yore. People of her generation, reared in apartments thought it was a mansion. Her father was in the Indian Administrative Service and had just become the Chief Secretary of one of the most prosperous states of India. What the heck, didn't Dalit mean 'oppressed'?

The windows slid open. The BMW had gone. It was a Saturday morning. Laundry and racquet game was an outline Mrs Rai sketched. Between chores and mental images, she would peek out of the window. No movement on the street, neither man nor bird. Her alley was a still life painting of an open-air screen.

Antana made sure the weekend was hectic. She took her mother to China Town. It was like a home-coming as it seemed as chaotic and lively as an Indian *bazaar.* Crowds, street stalls, food joints, noise and aromas of cooking. They had a meal that had generous helpings and was value for money in a fancy restaurant. Her mother wanted to buy gifts for friends back home. So, they strolled down streets selling all kinds of knick-knacks. At a stall where there was a pleasant young lady with a beautiful smile, Mrs Rai picked up bracelets that looked Western. The sales lady packed them in pretty crotchet bags. Pleased with her purchase, they went to a tea stall to try out bubble tea. They walked back home which was about 5 miles away but surprisingly not strenuous for Mrs Rai, who was usually averse to walking any distance more than a yard. Good walking shoes, excellent roads, very disciplined traffic and pleasant weather aided the usually reluctant walker. Also, she knew Antana was not keen on spending money on public transport. The girl had some admirable traits. She was conscious of the fact that her father had spent his nest-egg to send her to the Harvard of Canada. She was determined to use as little as she could on anything beyond necessities. The fact that she got a waiver of fees for the first year had thrilled her. She had worked hard to add value to her CV and all that helped her get into the only university she applied to. It obviously impressed them to give that fee waiver as well. Mrs Rai had wanted her to apply at Cornell but Antana balked at the thought of being in America. She refused to even apply for an American visa.

When they got back home, they took off their footwear and left it in the airing cupboard by the front door. Mrs Rai asked Antana if she wanted to use the washroom first. Antana let her mother use it, knowing how particular her parents were about washing hands, face and feet when they returned home from any outing.

That Monday morning, Antana again caught a snippet with caste reference to her father. The article was about how her father's great uncle, a minister in Bengal, had helped Dr Ambedkar(the Father of the Indian Constitution) get into the Drafting Committee of the Constitution of India. This time she came to her mother and asked point blank, "Why are they constantly referring to pa as a Dalit? Are we?" Her mother smiled and gently reminded her that she was a Christian like her mother. So, they were certainly not Dalits, and that her father's father was a Dalit. Her father's mother's family were Kulin Brahmins four generations ago. The great grandfather of her grandmother had been kicked out of his family for conversion. He had left Calcutta and moved up to Punjab, where he married a Kashmiri pandit who also converted to Christianity. They had built a Church in their part of Punjab. It was a tourist attraction.

"Gosh! I wrote papers in support of Dalits in college and had no clue I was one of them!"

"You are not and will never be," her mother snapped. "Your father got into the IAS in the general quota. It has no significance or relevance to our lives. I never knew anything about the Dalit connection when I married. For me, what was important was the Christian background. Your grandmother was a devout Christian who had major influence over your father who adored her... All this is just media hype and vested interests getting mileage."

Antana could not understand how her grandfather could be so devout if he was a Dalit. "Gandhiji had said that that the caste system was an excrescence and retrograde or something like that. To be an outcaste is the worst form of oppression, as bad as slavery," she said in utter contempt and asked if she could discuss this newly discovered heritage with her father. Her mother advised her not to. She told her that her grandmother was most upset when her brother-in-law who was Antana's grandfather's younger brother, also an ICS Officer, had written his memoirs, because he had mentioned his Namasudra background. The matriarch declared, "I have protected my children against this caste baggage in a caste-ridden society till now. Why did their uncle have to bring this up? The curse of wretched caste shall not be cast upon my children."

"Your aunt said she had never been told of this caste tag till some relative of the paternal side mentioned something, assuming they were all aware of the family caste. Aunt was then dating a rich guy from a business family. She thought that they would never accept a low caste girl as a daughter-in-law and she broke up. She converted to Christianity, much to your *Dadu's* dismay and your grandmother's delight. But it turned out well anyway, as she married Uncle Ram, a practicing Christian. He is a good husband, with impeccable educational degrees from IIT and MIT and hails from the royal family of Kapurthala. His grandfather's grandfather was a prince from there who converted to Christianity, was disinherited and displaced from the line to the crown but compensated with huge estates in a hill station. Uncle Ram and your aunt are also distant cousins because the ex- Prince married your great grandmother's aunt."

"Phew! So much convoluted family history that I was totally unaware of!" exclaimed Antana. "Oh well, good old Weber had dubbed our species as social products of race and class."

Either way, Antana was in a minority. Christians had none of the privileges and perks that the Scheduled Caste and Backward Class minority got as appeasement for vote banks in the guise of compensation for accidents of birth and the travesty of the system. Her mother advised her to concentrate on living in the first world where caste was irrelevant and attaining entry into the high class by dint of hard work and on her own merit would hold her in good stead. Into the bargain, she emphasized that equality was a myth

Her mother made pancakes and served it with maple syrup and blue berries. Antana left for the University.

Evening shadows fell after 9.30 pm. Neither of the men were seen. Dark clouds cast a gloom. Tuesday morning did not bring them back. "Maybe, BMW baba will not return," said Mrs Rai with a strange sense of foreboding. Antana assured her that he would. "Not before I leave," she thought aloud. Even the colours of the garden seemed to be fading. Blossom Baba's shiny black hair was styled like an upside-down tea cup or soup bowl. It suited him. She saw him stand on the 2nd floor balcony in a black kimono or karategi looking down at his garden.

One night after a thunder storm, she saw lights ablaze in BMW Baba's house. Diwali, at the end of July? Fireworks lit the sky from the old port. Antana smiled as her mother sighed contentedly and announced that she was off to bed. Mrs Rai rose and said, "I'm sure BMW Baba must miss home wherever it is. How lovely if we could invite him for an Indian meal before I leave. Good night, my precious girl."

At breakfast the next morning Mrs Rai told Antana that she had seen BMW Baba in a well-cut suit in a shade of charcoal grey with a baby blush pink shirt and a vibrant hued tie that could pass off for a Natya Baul creation. He probably owns the business or whatever. How else can he pop in and out of his home at such frequent intervals during a work day! The daughter, wise to local ways said, "you can even go for a swim, jig or jog during working hours. Where I worked last, a senior colleague did it every single day."

"Ah! I get it. It is like the officers in our building back home who take their own sweet time getting to work. I have seen lady officers at the beauty parlours, supermarket and the promenade during working hours. That friend of ours who is junior to your father used to go for a swim and work out at the club gym at noon even on working days."

"Yikes! No, no! Don't even try to draw allusions. Back home, the subtext is unaccountability. Ugh!" winced Antana.

That evening, Antana saw her mum's BMW Baba enter the back door of his house with a svelte, strawberry blonde leaning onto him. She thought there was no need to tell her mother. Glad that had escaped Mrs Rai's eyes, the young girl slid the windows firmly shut. She pulled the drapes across.

Men, inequality, love - life in continuum...

32

2

Wish Fulfillment

A glass chandelier, coloured blue like copper sulphate, was the spectacular centre piece. Suspended low from a white ceiling, it hung above an old rosewood table. Ten exquisite dining chairs had been salvaged from a shop in Chor Bazaar. The interior designer was one of the owners of that shop. She delved deep into the inventory to do up the apartment. An organza tablecloth with shadow-work embroidery was an ephemeral gossamer white on ivory. A delicate fragility, it was a metaphor for the transient. Some of the finest pieces were of the flawless craftsmanship of nimble fingers and delicate stitches. All of this was a part of the legacy of a foreign hand when Belgian and Irish nuns taught the poor local girls this needlecraft. The rich and Westernized, patronized the convents of South India when they made trousseaus for their daughters.

Sunflowers were exported to Europe by

Indians who planted them centuries ago. Tulips were over a thousand years of bloom in Turkey - a gift to Holland which became synonymous with the Dutch. It was even used as currency there till market forces ended 'Tulipmania'. When the Turks had to leave their former homeland in Eastern Europe, there were a few animals grazing in the fields. Pigs were very few because of the food taboo. Serbian pigs, wild pigs and these abandoned pigs intermingled and in the natural course, a new breed of mixed strain filled that land. They were the Mangalica pigs, easy to rear and farm. More recently, swine fever had decimated a few million.

Someone at the table flitted the conversation from swine to men. The topic of discussion was Arman Turch, more specifically how women found him irresistible and the K-factor in his life - from artist Kara to Kina , the Indian author. "Must be fond of K-babes," said one guest and laughed the loudest. "They spend considerable time in Goa these days. How much can one ever know about the anguish in another being?" the host said soulfully, quoting Turch. He added, "We have his book 'My name is Djed' for each of you as give-aways." Loud applause punctuated the dinner talk.

The hosts had just set up their Nation's Consulate General in Bombay. The couple was young and good looking, happy to be in the Island city.Their last posting had been at their embassy in New Delhi. They had settled in well at the spacious flat, which was actually two adjoining flats merged into one. Berat proudly announced that it was at the Consular Corps spouses' coffee morning sessions that Zehra had got a lead start to the property. They had cut through the middle man racket.

Berat and Zehra had been at university together studying International law. Both cleared the Foreign Service exams. When Berat proposed marriage, Zehra decided to forego a Foreign Service career. A capable and supportive wife is a great asset in any walk of life, more so in the diplomatic service. Working women without husbands usually do a marathon. One European diplomat traded her husband for a wife. The ex-husband subsequently became a popular writer of philosophical books and romantic poetry.

Zehra's works of art were pure magic. The camera was her muse and her photographs were beyond definition. She had turned her hobby into a part time business, and conducted classes and workshops. Since she was rarely in the photo frames that dotted their tables and very rarely in the pictures of family celebrations, she trained her husband to step in. He turned out to have a distinct style, very different from hers. Each one's personality was different too but complemented each other. Together they held an exhibition at a well-known gallery. The proceeds were donated to a local charity.

Berat took up a shot glass filled it with a clear

liquid from a bottle beside him on the table. The guests' shot glasses were filled. He requested them to first drink some water and then sip the contents of the shot glass. Raki was their National drink, which one of the guests described as adult gripe water. Aniseed was the main flavour, with notes of liquorice in strength of 70-80%. Raki was the Ouzo of the Greeks. They called it lion milk. "Serefe!" cheered Zehra and Berat. "Cheers!" the Indian guests returned.

'Havadan Sudan' by Ebru Yasar played in the background. Yasar was an attractive singer with a husky voice. One of the guests asked what it meant. "Like air and water, a simile for small talk," explained Zehra. Small talk was an idiom for the cocktail circuit and diplomacy rubbing shoulders with civil society at social events. A couple of years later when they were in the process of consolidating what they had started, out of the blue came orders for Berat to take up the post of an Ambassador in a country among the Pacific Islands. The children were very upset as was Zehra, who had made her mark in the city as a photographer and a woman of substance. Berat was the first in his batch to be promoted as Ambassador. He left within a week of the orders being issued. Zehra and the children stayed back to finish the academic year. Close to their departure date Berat instructed them to change direction. Zehra had to get the tickets cancelled and flew to Istanbul instead.

Two months later news came that Berat had

filed for divorce. People who knew them found it hard to believe. It was an ugly and acrimonious split with no refinement of endings. He divorced the two beautiful children as well. They were eight and twelve that year. Stunned friends scattered around the world, uttered a single word, 'Nazar' over and over in different conversations.

The next Consul General posted in Berat's place was Nil Kemal. She had a four-year-old Turkish Van. Getting a Visa for her cat was a complicated process, so, she waited at Istanbul. One evening as she was walking along the Bosphorus Bridge, she ran into some old friends. They introduced her to their friend. The two hit it off from the word 'Merhaba'. Over cups of Turkish coffee and Kumpir potato they discovered that a Tarot card reader had told Tan that his next wife would be someone involved with international relations. The uncanny part was that the woman she had described was in the image of Nil. Destiny played out its hand. After their government had vetted and approved, Nil and Tan were married in the Embassy at Delhi. The ambassador officiated the ceremony, and by the powers vested in him, joined them in holy matrimony. The wedding gift included a honeymoon package to the Taj Mahal. In due course, she proceeded on maternity leave and the baby was given an Indian name.

Adlee Ozbey succeeded Nil. Deniz and Adlee brought with them charming candour and warmth. While Adlee, attractive like most Turks, was a workaholic. He was also a devoted family man. His wife Deniz was a friendly, petite and pretty brunette. She did decoupage on furniture and knick- knacks. Her work was very neat with hints of her being a perfectionist. This couple was natural and fresh like the Turkish delight and hazelnuts they always served at their home with Turkish coffee. Their home was in the famed Sea Palace building at Malabar Hill, overlooking the Arabian Sea. They quietly and discreetly did a lot of charity work. Adlee, an avid art collector, patronised local artists. They were liberal, broadminded, fair and just in their dealings and he, the model diplomat in a very real sense.

Turkey was brought to Bombay in myriad ways - food festivals, art exhibitions, Sufi music and dervishes. Rumi's direct descendent, a beautiful and gracious lady who headed the International Mevlana Foundation, had given lectures at Bombay University. Deniz even put up a souvenir stall and a Turkish coffee stall selling coffee and mezze. Deniz had personally made the food items with a couple of Turkish officers of the Consulate, for a pre- Diwali mela that wives' associations of high ranking government officers had organized. They had integrated well with all; their household staff adored them. The Consulate General's local staff wept at the farewell hosted for Adlee and Deniz. Adlee had been promoted to go as an Ambassador to the Turks and Caicos. Indian friends and Consular Corps colleagues felt the pangs of parting, and the rumblings of partying non-stop for three weeks echoed at every one of the multiple farewell parties hosted for this popular couple.

A few months after Adlee took up his Ambassador post, he extended an invitation to an Indian couple who knew his predecessors. The Indian friend was touched that Adlee had kept his word. It had been his wife's much longed for wish to visit Turkey. Her father was supposed to take up a posting there but as she was in her final year of school, he bowed out of that position and even changed jobs so that her studies were not interrupted. The man sent his wife alone with a very generous allowance. Instead of USD he bought Euros which were more expensive.

Deniz and Zehra had never met, but collaborated closely to coordinate the visit of their 'Aapa'(elder sister). The Indian woman had insisted they call her that instead of madam when they first met. Deniz had to flit between Ankara and Cockburn Town. Their young daughter was schooling at Ankara. Deniz had chosen to do a T tour. A dekko at the map of Tukey outlines Istanbul, Ankara and Konya in the shape of a calligraphic T. She had booked tickets on a luxury bus for the Istanbul to Ankara stretch, and a train ride by business class from Ankara to Konya, the land of Rumi and Sufi.

The Turkish Airlines upgraded Aapa to Business class when they learnt she was the guest of one of their ambassadors. Aapa was thrilled. The luxury of her upgrade and the comfort of the cabin lulled her into a deep sleep. She woke up ninety minutes before landing and lapped up from above the earth the scenic beauty below. Deniz flew in from Ankara on an early morning flight to receive Aapa. Zehra, now an acclaimed photographer had rescheduled shoots so that she could take the two visitors around her beloved Istanbul for two days.

The three women met and embraced each other like soul sisters. Such little time, so much to do, say, see: centuries of history, cross cultures of East and West, modernity and tradition and beauty in people, stone, tile, sea, hills, trees and riots of colour spread on the ground in the national flower outburst. Many lifetimes encapsulated in every moment. Aapa was in the moment, and she wished the moment could last forever.

From tombs and mosques to roof top cafes, green trees, Bosphorus blown breeze, delicious Turkish meals, shopping, trudging up hilly roads and sliding down slopes, tripping, laughter, sharing, caring and listening, to Zehra's incredible knowledge of her intercontinental city. Seas of tulips, hyacinths, and daffodils became colour blocked imprints etched in memory. Several cups of Damla Turkish coffee, baklava, mezze, little glasses of Turkish tea, and ultimately the cruise down the Bosphorus that was flanked by Europe and Asia was a sail with an interesting tale through every nautical mile. They passed the military academy that was now an empty monument; the bombed-out building left in its ruins. The waterfront mansions of the wealthy, pine trees which bore the chilgoza nuts, and the Judas trees in blushing violet, soon to be lost in the subconscious now lay at the tip of the mind.

By metro they went to see Zehra's studio. It was a 2000 square feet hall she discovered by networking. She had turned it to a poly-design studio. She shared space and rental with three others - an architect, a web-designer and a painter of still life and portraits. Zehra's touches could be seen in every nook and cranny. Lots of India placed here and there was heart-warming for Aapa. Zehra generously did some portrait pictures of Deniz and Aapa. With the timer, she took a beautiful shot of the three of them. Aapa, shyly said, "Thank you Zehra! Such a nice way to crystallize this holiday that both of you have curated specially for me, my dearest Deniz and Zehra." A rich harvest of memories would be reaped by the hour, to last till memory was alive to replay.

At the Spice Bazar, Aapa shopped for everything - from Sumac, chilli paste, hazel nuts, walnuts, dried raspberries, figs and lemon strips, to tahini paste, zaatar, halva and coffee. Only when the bill was made did all three realize that they were in an Egyptian store. At a jewellery shop, Aapa bought an evil eye charm bracelet made of silver and dipped in gold. Before they caught a tram back to the hotel, they stopped for supper at a popular restaurant. As they broke bread, Zehra told them that Berat's new wife, older than her, had filed a law suit to stop alimony payments. She won the case on grounds that Zehra, now 'an acclaimed photographer of the country was rolling in Turkish Lira.' The Court directed Zehra to pay Berat 7250 USD as reverse alimony! Horrified, Aapa and Deniz in unison cried out, "Don't!"

Zehra asked Deniz if she knew how much an ambassador's pay was. Berat was in the African Continent which meant a higher allowance. Deniz was clueless. All that Berat paid as monthly childcare allowance was a total of 300USD. The kids lost out on a parent who was alive and kicking in dollars. Berat had recently visited Istanbul with his wife. He invited the kids over and spent a scant forty minutes with them as the couple had to attend a family wedding. He took a selfie with the fruits of his loins, gave them dinner money, and packed them off promising them a Play Station and vinyl record player before he left. That was the last they saw or heard of him. The son, ever hopeful, would come back from school expecting to see the promised gifts. This went on for about seven months till he figured it was not to be. "Still, he hopes it will arrive for his birthday in July," said Zehra with a sigh. Deniz asked her if he had been a good father in happier times. Without any hesitation, Zehra indicated that he was. Deniz then related her personal story of how she and her little brother were raised by scheming relatives because of her parents' ugly divorce. She had only bad memories of her father and the terror of him selling his half of their home to some stranger. She broke down, which opened the flood gates of tears among all three. Deniz rushed to the washroom. Zehra turned to Aapa and said, "Some hurt never goes away. I would never have imagined happy go lucky Deniz having such a past. It haunts you all your life. My children have been traumatized. I fear that their relationships will be difficult in adult life. No matter how hard I try, I cannot be substitute for a father. Someday I may meet a man I want to spend the rest of my life with but that will not mean my children get a father..."

Deniz returned to the table all red in the face, as if she had tried to scrub away all traces of her hidden pain and sorrow the other two had been allowed a sneak peek at. Briskly she asked Zehra to guide her about the following day's programme. But Zehra had a full day of photo shoots at different locales. She could not join them. A tram season Pass from her bag was given to Deniz. Zehra drew a map of sorts on the back of her business card. The Blue Mosque, Hagia Sophia and Topkapi Palace were on the agenda.

Aapa hugged Zehra tight and thanked her for a wonderful time. Zehra said she would try to meet them the next evening but could not promise anything. Aapa refused that offer saying that she should not worry about coming over after a full day's work. She hoped to see her in Bombay someday. As Deniz and Zehra hugged, they whispered to each other 'Gecmisolsun', which conveyed the hope that the bad times and bad things be relegated to the past. Aapa thought it takes just a fraction of a nanosecond to alter the state of 'IS' to 'WAS'.

After a lavish breakfast at the buffet served in their hotel, Deniz and Aapa made an early start for the Blue Mosque. Adlee had laughed at the stupidity of trying to visit the Blue Mosque on a Friday. Deniz had never ventured out alone in Istanbul ever before. She was nervous. Aapa felt guilty that she could be of no use. Little Deniz squared her slender shoulders, took Aapa's hand and said, "Come, let us brave the sights and sounds on our own today." To ease the stress, Aapa suggested they do just the Blue Mosque. Deniz vetoed her suggestion.

As they stepped out of the Metro station and crossed the road to the Blue Mosque, a Chador clad Asian Turk stopped to admire Aapa's attire and complimented her. Aapa smiled and said it was from India. The young lady asked if she were Indian and Aapa said she was. "Wonderful!" exclaimed the stranger. Like ships that pass each other by night they crossed over in opposite directions.

At the Blue Mosque, Aapa prayed for all especially her host families. Ever since Zehra's turn of fate, she never failed to say a prayer for her and the children every now and then. Deniz and Adlee were special people and she thanked God for them and to bless them and theirs. Who would have thought that the beautiful mosque was a four-hundred-year-old structure? It looked fresh and new like morning dew.

Seeing the serpentine queue that was at least a mile long, Aapa urged Deniz to skip it. Deniz made Aapa stand before her, behind a Chinese lady. They were probably hundredth in line. Deniz told Aapa that Adlee had expressly ordered her to bring Aapa to Hagia Sophia. A plainclothes official who overheard Deniz came up to them and asked her something in Turkish. Before Aapa realized what was happening, the official was leading them to the ticketing window. Amazing Grace she thought aloud. Deniz smiled and said it was a big relief to jump the queue. She thanked the kind man graciously.

Adlee, back in Bombay had told Aapa about the Muslim- Catholic shrine called Meryemana Evi – the House of Mother Mary. Since Ephesus was not part of the T tour, he had made a visit to this remarkable holy place at Istanbul mandatory. Aapa could feel the sanctity of this ancient Byzantine edifice. Despite the people, the hum of different tongues, the black cat crouched under a column like a sinister figure in an Alfred Hitchcock movie, the scaffolding, and the flash of cell phone cameras, there was a kind of hush and reverence that engulfed her. Here was a testament to human ingenuity. How much labour must have gone into its making? The physical man-made world has been built by the poverty stricken and hungry. What was the brain that designed this and how was it humanly possible to execute such proportions? They could not fathom what machinery was employed in those ancient times to construct something that stood the test of time despite destruction over and over again. From Christian to Greek Orthodox to Roman Catholic to Greek Orthodox to mosque to museum it remained eternally sacred, in Holy Wisdom. Such mystical glory reflected in the colours. The repairs and restoration were a work in progress, never ceasing, never complete. The splendour of human endeavour, divinely ordained, was the only way Aapa could fathom this creation. Deniz and Aapa both agreed that the structures and architecture of modern day would not stand the test of time. "The glass and chrome buildings towering the Bombay skyline are sky high disasters. They are as artificial as the people who live in them," said Aapa giddily.

At the "Wishing Column" there was a short queue. Aapa took a place at the end of the line. She watched the ones ahead turn their thumbs 360 degrees in the hole covered by bronze plates. When her turn came she stuck her thumb in, closed her eyes made a wish and turned her thumb but mid-way it got stuck. She looked at Deniz in panic. Pulling her thumb out, shaken, she moved away. A strange disquiet descended upon her. Not wanting to dwell in the moment, she told Deniz that they should go to the Museum store for some retail therapy.

At the Topkapi Palace, the atmosphere was

different and both women let their hair down. At the harem quarters, they tried to imagine the hordes of nubile sex slaves brought in from all parts to give good stock to the Ottoman Empire. The jealousies and intrigue were now sealed in the stone walls and buried deep beneath the floors. The gardens and the beautiful palace rooms were a distracting pleasure trip. They sat in the open area of the Konyali Palace restaurant and had a sumptuous lunch. Aapa had ordered a kabab meal. She was taken aback to see slabs of cooked lamb instead of kebabs, so Deniz exchanged the seekh kebab on her platter for the lamb. Aapa, overcome by the fuzzy warmth of Deniz's caring, the beautiful ambience and rush of pheromones, impulsively suggested they do a trip to Berlin the following year. Both of them had a friend who had been posted to Berlin before Adlee's transfer orders came. (Aapa in her mind calculated that she would be able to save the bulk of her Euros for the next holiday. Her husband had been uncharacteristically generous with her foreign travel allowance.) Deniz said it was an idea but she would have to discuss it with Adlee before they made plans.

They decided to end the day's excursion with a trip to the grand bazar. On the way, Deniz stopped to ask for directions to the bazar. The young men she asked shrugged and conveyed in broken English that they did not speak Turkish but could help if she spoke English. They were enthusiastic to help once they understood. At the Bazaar, Aapa gawked at the gold souk. The love for gold equalled the Indian penchant for the yellow metal. She bought another evil eye charm bracelet in gold. Deniz refused her offer of a gift of an identical piece. Aapa thought she would give Deniz 200 Euros in Ankara to buy whatever caught her fancy. They headed back to the hotel in a tram packed like sardines. As they alighted and at the crossroads, Deniz, thrilled that they had pulled off a fabulous day, took a selfie of the two happy tourists. Like little girls they did a hop, skip and jump as they trilled Uskudara Giderken.

The grand finale was seeing Zehra waiting for them at the lobby of their boutique hotel near Galata Towers. They hugged each other in a warm embrace. Aapa announced that she would take them out to dinner. Zehra said she had just dropped in for a short while and had to head home sooner than later. So Aapa quickly suggested that they skip going up to the room to freshen up. Instead, they used the facilities at the lobby level. Zehra was asked to lead the way to a swish restaurant with good food and wine. Aapa told her sylph-like friends that 'balik etli' in their language, meant fish fleshed. And she wanted them to get curvier. They burst into giggles like adolescent girls in an all-girls' school. They discussed their day out. Zehra asked Aapa whether she had made a wish at the Wishing Column. With a beatific smile Aapa said solemnly, "I wished that all get wealth." They whooped joyously. A money changing centre was open.

Aapa wanted to change a few hundred Euros. She reached out for her little shoulder bag which to her surprise had the zipper open. She put her hand in. It was a cold cavity.

The wallet was never found. It had credit and debit cards, a gold coin from the Vatican blest by the Pope and over a month's salary that her husband had converted to Euros. He had said, "This is your much wished for holiday. Go enjoy!"

'Nazar Degmesin' is a Turkish phrase which when translated means, 'May you not be touched by the evil eye.'

3

The Agony Aunt

Jumping ahead of herself Avia thought, to take what one can while the going is good is a skirmish won. In many expressions of life and love there is none more graphic than a deep sigh. Some neuron transmitter triggered off a long sigh in Avia.

Rational Emotive Behaviour Therapy and other new age safeguards had sprung up in the mind springs of health. Anti-inflammatory balms for mind and body were pedaled by new age therapists and quacks. But if they worked, fie! to the sceptical or cynical. When Avia got her REBT certificate, she headed the queue for an internship at the doctor's chamber. The deal was that she would not earn but would gain from the sprightly doctor's wisdom, experience, archives and good will. In any case, it would be a refreshing and pleasant change from being just a tele-marketer.

The interns were given a certain number of

letters/queries to sort out. Anything beyond their depth would be pushed up to the good doctor himself. The interns got to do the "Dear Other" column that dealt with the general. The doctor dealt with the specifics of sexual disorders or dilemmas in the 'Sexpertix' column.

In her debut, Avia addressed a young girl's query of how to stop nail chewing. She advised her to soak her nails in neem oil every morning. Another tip was to go to a nail bar and get her nails artistically done so that the nailed art work would distract her from cannibalising it.

Avia, staring out of the window after sending the needful to the editorial team online, was chewing on her toe nails, an old habit. She always found it comforting, and this way kept her hands neatly manicured. Her exasperated mother called it the most disgusting foot and mouth disease.

The longer she worked on the queries, the more her wonder grew about quirks, fears, anxieties, and the human predicament. There was something rare about common sense. A distressed man wrote that as he was sleeping in the nude, pigeons try to nestle over the wardrobe had flown in and their droppings had fallen on crucial parts of his lower body? Would it affect his libido or make him sterile? Avia kept that query aside for her boss.

Going through the files in the archives, she found it to be a veritable treasure trove. The doctor's advice read more like 'laughter is the best medicine' column. Avia's friends' mums saw her as a role model. They marvelled at her maturity in handling some queries. When she bumped into some of these ladies they had a volley of questions she had to field. One day Dr Seksaria, her boss, asked her to address a fairly long one.

"I am twenty years old, blissfully married for the last two years to a handsome and loving man chosen by my parents. We live abroad. In our apartment building are mainly Asians and we have become friendly with many. Our immediate neighbour belongs to one of our neighbouring countries. We have been to a few parties of common contacts. The other night after a party, my husband offered the friend whose wife and kids are on vacation a lift home. So while my husband sat in front with the driver, he insisted that the pal share the back seat with me. Half way home, the friend put his hand across my shoulder. I was not comfortable and started squirming. He did not seem to notice but did nothing else. I moved as far as I could and was on the edge. My husband, oblivious, was chatting away. If the driver had noticed, there was nothing he could do anyway.

A few days later the same neighbour rang my door bell and seemed to be in a panic. The shirt he was wearing had the collar button off and he stood there with the button and tie in the other hand. He asked me if I could sew it back as his wife had not returned from her parental home. I promptly proceeded to do as he asked. Quickly, I threaded a needle and it seemed easier to get it over and done with while he wore the shirt. I told him to stand still. He did and I quickly stitched the button back. He thanked me profusely and left. A few weeks later he rushed in with a more stricken look. This time it was the belt loop on his trousers. So, I stepped into the bedroom of our tiny single bedroom apartment, with the man. I sent him to the bathroom with instructions to hand over the trousers while he waited there. I quickly stitched it on. He dressed up and left showering me with thanks. That very day I happened to mention these episodes to a resident of the building. She told me that the man was a philanderer and that the poor wife had walked out on him this time. She advised me to withhold these encounters from my husband. I now shudder to think of my husband's reaction had he walked into the house and found the half-dressed man without pants in our bathroom. I feel I should tell my husband. What should I do?"

"A stitch in time saved your neighbour. A frank conversation with your husband about the friendly neighbour is advisable. 'Love thy neighbour' is a tenet best reserved for the worthy ones. Another man in the master bathroom with his pants down may put the kibosh on a happy marriage. You are young and innocent. Why let a wolf in damaged clothing pull the wool over your eyes?" Avia went to show her boss. Dr Seksaria liked the response. Like a butterfly, Avia floated out of his chamber.

Sitting at the Head 2 Toes Salon, Avia was

getting a pedicure. She checked the papers. Her colleague, the other intern had worked on a query that got featured.

"I am what they call a 'late bloomer'. I attained menarche only seven months ago. I am sixteen now. People mistake me for a seventh grader! Two days ago, my elder brother's friend who has known us for the last three years was in the lift with me and there was no one else. He suddenly asked me if we could kiss. I dumbly nodded. It was my first time ever. When he drew me close and put his lips on mine, something sticky oozed into my panty and I thought I had started my periods again. It was not. Now, every time I relive the episode, the same thing happens. Is there something wrong? Could I be pregnant?"

"Dear late bloomer,

No need to panic. These are natural body reaction and secretion to such stimuli. Read 'Growing up and the Body Manual' by Dr Seksaria."

The Salon attendant then persuaded her to go for a manicure too. Avia gave up reading. Just then her phone started ringing but she shut it out. Her mother had been trying her number and she sent Avia a message: *Urgent! Come home asap. Don't worry, we are okay.*

Avia rushed home after her salon session. In the drawing room were a couple of strangers sitting with her parents. Avia was introduced to the young couple who were distant relatives of her mother's aunt-in-law. They seemed pleasant and struck up a lively conversation about nothing in particular. After a half hour or so, they took their leave. Her mother asked them if they would come again and they assured her they would certainly do that. Probably, sooner than later, they added. Avia's mum looked smug and saw them off -right up to the gate. Avia picked up her bag from the sofa and headed for her room. She had work to do.

1. "Blood edged- lust is what drives my new boyfriend. His routine is that we smoke some grass after a shot of Absinthe. He then makes me stand against a wall with my hands raised up and flicks a fresh blunt blade through a red, padded leather jacket he drapes on me. There are no cuts or nicks on my arms yet. I am not sure if I should stay or quit. He is otherwise, bright, a brilliantly good conversationalist,nice looking, generous and is doing his thesis on conflict resolution and pacifism. This seems to be the only kink so far. Should I stay or quit ahead of a blood bath or sanguine end?"

'Love by 100 cuts makes a good book title or cinematographer's file noting' was an aside Avia sent along with the query to the doctor.

2. "My husband goes abroad often with official delegations. His boss rounds up juniors, after working hours and takes them out to a lavish meal followed by visits to weird

places. X-rated night clubs are a hot spot. Once when they got back, my husband brought home a few black ping pong balls and asked me to try to squeeze them in one at a time within my vaginal walls through a kegel type exercise. The most recent trip was where a nude performer lay on a silk satin covered dining table and was transformed to an organic dish. My husband now wants to have crepe suzettes slathered in honey off me. He experiments with a different menu every weekend. Will all this cause infection and indigestion?"

3. "My boss is trying to harass me into sexual subjugation. It is awful but I need the job. My husband is trying to cajole me into submission. He says it is every man's fantasy to see his wife doing it with another woman. I'd rather turn into a prostitute, where I can probably earn more and doing it with men far more pleasurable than with a woman. The very thought makes me sick. If it were not for my two-year-old twins, I'd kill myself. HELP!"

4. "My homophobic partner wants to try out a threesome. I am "lesbophobic" myself. What should we do? What is Kamadeva rati-sadhana?"

Avia filed them away for the sexpert. The next day Avia's mother told her that she had invited the couple who had visited earlier, for dinner.

Avia had to help with dessert and a couple of salads. She made a broccoli and bacon salad, Thai green papaya and a sugar free steamed yoghurt dessert.

Rama and Jana were the couple she had met. They came with a very handsome young man. Avia gawked when she saw him. When he opened his mouth and a strong baritone voice greeted her, she thought this was some rock star. He was introduced as Abiram Rakey. He was an entomologist posted at Takeymanore, Avia's favourite hill station. She felt a magnetic attraction to this hunk. She spent the rest of the evening being the most attentive hostess. When Abiram asked her if he could call her up later, she gave him her mobile and landline numbers to be absolutely sure that call would be made.

Abiram called her up every day for a fortnight and then informed her that he would be in town for the weekend and would like to meet her. Avia was ecstatic. That Friday evening was exciting as Abiram took her out for dinner to her favourite restaurant. When he dropped her home, they fixed up a movie date for the following day. By Sunday, Avia's parents asked her if she liked Abiram as his people had sent a wedding proposal. For Avia, it was a dream come true. Before it all sank in, the wedding date had been fixed.

The next few weeks were a whirlwind of shopping and fittings at the tailor. Avia was sent to her aunt in the big city to do some trousseau shopping and buy her wedding outfit. Her father chose the very expensive Bollywood dress designer to do his *laadli beti's* wedding clothes. He wanted the wedding to be the talk of the town for years to come. "Even my grandchildren should hear about how I had arranged my only girl's big day. As a banker, we invest in mega deals and a marriage is a long-term relationship that I shall spare no cost to invest in. Getting a son-in-law like Abiram is a priceless value addition."

As promised, her father made his grandiose plan a well-executed grand event. The scale and lavishness of it all was the talk of the town. A Jungle theme with *mashaals* and a fibre glass jungle-scape was the venue design. There were waiters dressed like apes and bears bearing trays of high calorie bite size snacks, and barbecue spits with tantalizing aromas. Tulips, lavender sprays and orchids were ordered from the imported flower dealer up north. The live band had 'gorillas and tigers' playing. The guests were floored but a tad disappointed that the bride and groom were not dressed like Tarzan and Jane. The father of the bride arranged for two honeymoons. One to the Maldives and the other to South Africa. Though the wedding Invitations had "No presents, only blessings" printed on them, many blessings in silver and gold were showered upon the newlyweds. Envelopes piled up too.

The wedding night was spent opening up a room full of gifts. After the double destination honeymoon, the couple returned to Avia's home town. Abiram had to re-join duty immediately. He gave Avia the option of spending a month or less with her parents before joining him. She chose a fortnight as she was eager to join him. He left, promising to get the little quarter spruced up for his beloved bride. Avia marvelled at her luck. Her friends thought she had hit pay dirt.

Abiram came in a jeep to take his bride back. Avia was on top of the world and her parents were so pleased that their daughter was glowing with happiness. The first night in the little barrack at the Research Centre was so romantic. Power outages were common, and the candle light seemed to make it so ethereal, like the fairy tales she used to devour as a child.

Alogard, the faithful Man Friday she had heard so much about from Abiram was on leave. He would be back in a week, Abiram mentioned. He reassured her that things would be perfect when he returned from the village.

Their first week was tender and loving. Abiram said he respected her so much that he would not be some savage stranger who exercised his conjugal rights just because they were legally married. Avia thought that was the most romantic and considerate allowance any man could make. Their honeymoon had been a holiday of exploring sea, land and wildlife.

The week flew by and Alogard returned from the village. Avia was surprised to find he was a young lad of about 18 and not some wise old man as she had assumed. Abiram had asked her to rustle up dinner for all three as the boy had arrived late that evening and looked tired. After dinner, Abiram seemed distant and pre-occupied. Avia asked him if there was some work-related issue. He shrugged it off. She hugged him tight and said good night as she went to her single twin bed. Their beds had a smaller dresser between them just as the ones in the hotel they stayed in. Abiram had told her that the Mahogany king size bed he had ordered was not ready. Till then they would keep the room as it was. Avia blushed at the thought of their marital king size bed. Abiram had a fine sense of aesthetics and she liked the way he had done it up. Abiram got into his bed and turned off the lights.

At some point closer to the break of dawn, Avia felt a draught and got up to pull the bedsheet open. She noticed that Abiram was not in bed. Extricating herself from the net covered bed, she paddled softly to the bathroom. It was not occupied so she went in. On her way back, she noticed doors of the other bedroom shut. She went to check. It was locked. She knocked but it went unanswered, she banged hard and harder and then shouted out, "Open the door".

Finally, the door opened and Abiram looked irritated and hissed, "What the hell! Why are you creating a ruckus?"

Stunned, Avia angrily pushed him aside and like a streak of lightning stormed into the room.

Cowering in the corner was young Alogard, draped in the sheet she had embroidered for the bottom drawer.

4

Carry the Can

Had she kept her eyes wide open, would it have been any different?

Ares used to walk her back from school in their final year. They were always in step as they walked, even though he was a 6-footer and she was several inches shorter. Sara was a couple of months short of her twentieth birthday, and Ares was all of twenty one when they wed. In school he had always been ahead of the others in class. At the staff room they called him A Plus. He used to coach Sara, and helped her get better grades. Five years of married life and Ares would rib her that he lost his bachelors while she gained a master. He earned his way into the finest temples of learning and all these value additions turned out to be the passwords to the corporate caves.

Ares and Sara moved on a foreign posting. There were neither major cultural shocks nor major adjustments required; life was in many ways easier than back in their home country. But as expats there was always a nagging yearning for their roots and a sense of belonging, nostalgia for food, places and people of the past.

Sara's two ectopic pregnancies that required medical termination brought them to terms with being a childless family. Sara thought that if her womb were hostile to life it meant she was not fit to be a mother. Instead of brooding, one weekend she impulsively decided to volunteer at a nearby crèche. A background check was run on her, two eminent citizens of the neighbourhood had to give testimonials supporting her, and only then was she considered for a proper interview. All this happened within the span of a fortnight, and then she was taken in as a volunteer.

Two months into her voluntary work, the stark truth that little ones were better in photographs and movies dawned on her. Parenthood was a demanding lifetime role. She patted her lifeless womb and thanked the higher powers for keeping her unborn children in a better place somewhere. Her part-time mothering role, time-bound for about four hours daily, sated her maternal urge. One mother related how her middle daughter aged four had picked up her half-eaten plate and emptied it into a Tupperware box. She then presented it to her mother to send to starving children in whatever part of the world necessary, as she was tired of hearing, "Finish the food you have been served and be grateful that you are not a starving child in some poor part of the world."

When she felt smothered, Sara called it quits. Coincidentally, soon after, Ares had to take up an assignment in Asia. Ares and Sara were now grappling with a whole new world. In the boondocks, Ares had to create an integrated campus for the fledgling ecological conservation project. It was trumpeted as a pioneering endeavour for a model ideal township. They were creating urban spaces in rural areas. Macro-ambition and economic theories were being tested to redefine parameters and alter images of mindset, landscape and social structure.

Ares, always passionate in whatever he undertook, found the new challenges inspiring and went whole hog. His passion, enthusiasm, charisma and compassion separated him from the rest. He was driven.

Predictably, Sara felt alienated. She began turning inward and more withdrawn. Apart from a couple of other expats there was not much other company. For Ares, trading personal time for professional games seemed like a win-win. He bought her expensive trinkets, and took her to Hong Kong and Macau often. Phuket and other Thai treasures were among the top getaways they frequented. Sara, never a big spender, enjoyed casino time and often made more than she spent.

An occasional drinker, Sara now started having her daily wine in red. It calmed her down and the tipple was soporific. She slept longer and was usually asleep when Ares left for work. Soon they seemed to orbit in different time zones.

Whatever Ares undertook consumed his energy and he paid great attention to detail. His outstanding personality traits made him larger than life. Sara's DNA made her the chiaroscuro in their marriage portrait. In the middle of nowhere she had no friends or family for company. Ares had an Annexe built and converted to a mini Las Vegas casino. Sara had no clue what was happening till he threw it open for her after leading her blindfolded to the unveiling of 'Las Sara Casina'.

Many happy hours were spent idling away in her custom-made casino. Wine and game made her world rosy hued. The local maid was trained to rustle up simple meals of their liking. Sara taught her a spot of baking of cakes, shortbread, scones and a basic brownie. She soon decided that the cook was far more talented than she was with pots and pans over the kitchen fire and recused herself from such messy duties.

The other wives envied Sara's life. Jet setter Ares was always showering her with expensive baubles from different parts of the world. Curios encased in Mahogany cabinets and on gilt edged marble tops. Rugs and kilims lay scattered around, but the magnificent Kashmiri carpet in black, coffee brown, rust and peacock blue with deep rose, a very unusual piece that covered the floor of the ante room was the show stopper. Her locker was brimming over with trinkets in jade,

South Sea pearls, and diamonds set in platinum in rings, earrings and bracelets. Rubies and sapphires sourced from Sri Lanka, and emeralds from Pakistan were lying in pouches waiting to be set.

Ares kept himself fighting fit. He was at the gym after work and on weekends played tennis followed by golf on Sunday afternoons. He did not seem to notice or mind that Sara had let herself go. Others thought she was sloppy and of an inferior class compared to Ares' Greek God stature. If he did not mind her frowzy appearance, he had begun noticing personality changes. He felt responsible for dragging her down. The more their bank balance grew, the more abandoned she felt.

Her amateur water colour paintings that she did at "Arty Sis" sessions were getting intensely morbid. It appeared as though she was so inside her experience that the colours were deepening into fiendish shades and the images turning into shadows. The associational life that she once craved for was now beginning to suffocate her.

Ares, with his big booming voice always filled with good humour automatically turned soft and gentle when he spoke of his wife. A tone of deep affection was always how he spoke with her. When he lost his temper with her on rare occasions, his voice merely turned raspy. Sara who was always a quiet person became quieter, and Ares taking stock decided they both required therapy. Sara, resentful, found communicating with the therapist exceedingly hard.

Ares began to spend more time in the board room and Sara inversely spent longer in bed living in a hypo-reality. The therapist suggested Ares slow down, take time off and whisk her away to a sunny place by the sea closer to their home country. The plan worked and he could see glimpses of the girl he had fallen so deeply in love with twenty odd years ago. A week at the resort and it was unbelievable, her transformation back to the girl Ares once spent every day with. The melancholy of the recent past had vaporised.

Sara absorbed the translucence and luminosity of shared passion and his deep abiding love. She decided to go for an overhaul. Sara signed up for a detox and rejuvenation programme at a spa resort. After a ten-day session there, on their recommendation she flew to a Naturopathy and Ayurvedic Centre in the country of its origin. Every time she lay on the wooden bench at the sauna, she imagined it would be a very similar experience in her final journey at the crematorium.

It was intensive. After a physical and mental rehaul, she was good to go; she had been away from Ares for weeks. A gradual descent into a normal world took place as her plane landed.

In her inward journey she battled all the self-absorption that had consumed her. Thanking her good fortune for having a man as special as Ares, she vowed she would do all to be worthy of his devotion and care. He deserved a better wife for all that he had done for her ever since she was sixteen. She chastised herself and did a bit of virtual self-flagellation at having taken so much for granted.

Ares had apologised for not being there to receive her. He had to attend a seminar at Nijmegen. With a tinkle of laughter and in a tone that Ares had not heard in a long time, Sara said, "Hey! My Greek god, you are the Ares, battling strife in the corporate world." Perhaps, he would surprise her with an early return.

Back home, Sara slept a deep sleep. At the crack of dawn, she heard the rumble of the gates open and a car drive up. She jumped out of bed and rushed to the bathroom to freshen up. When she emerged, she peeped out of the window and saw him standing on the lawn with his back to her. Maybe he had a call to make, she thought.

She got back in bed and smiled to herself. Settling down under silver grey satin sheets, she shut her eyes. Drifting off to sleep, she woke with a start to find the bedroom door ajar and caught a glimpse of Ares striding past the hallway.

The strident ringing of the doorbell made her scramble out of bed in search of her dressing gown. By the time she found it and tied the sash, the maid, dishevelled, looking as pale as the sheet on the bed stuttered that there were some visitors from Ares' office. Her sense of urgency seemed misplaced. Ares would sort it out, she thought. Sara hurriedly moved to the hall where she recognized two of Ares' junior colleagues. With them was a stranger with a black bag and they looked grimly anxious.

With a bright smile, Sara went up to them. Before, she could ask them to seat themselves, the older of the two colleagues took the lead. He led her to the sofa and gently sitting her down told her in a low voice, "Ares is in hospital, in the ICU."

She stared blankly and in a loud unfamiliar voice shouted, "No! He is home now!" Had she not seen him on the lawn and walk past…?

Darkness swamped her body as Sara felt herself descending, flakes of dust spilling out of a Grecian urn. Had she kept her eyes open, she wondered…

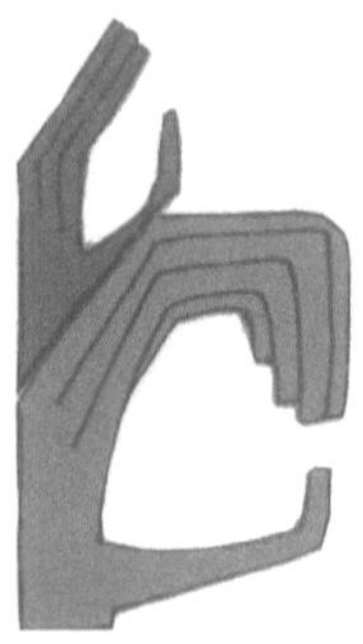

5

Sleight of hand

Raj's younger daughter had got into a Medical college last year. A belated celebration party combined with an overseas friend's visit was organized at his flat. Sharvee, giving us a virtual tour and orientation of life on campus, got animated about her curriculum, especially anatomy class. It was ghoulish. When she left the room, her father quickly confessed that his wife was nagging him to pull strings for hostel accommodation. Ever since she brought home the skeletal remains of a pair of human hands, her mother was in a tizzy about human remains defiling the home. The hot kebabs and crumb coated Bombay duck suddenly seemed less palatable.

A beaming Sharvee returned with the bony hands on an enamel tray. Those hands once belonged to someone real with flesh, sinew, skin and blood. Goose bumps appeared on my arms and I tried to still a shudder. Whose hands and what had they done in that lifetime?

Ironically, just that morning in the play group, an assistant teacher had asked the three-year-old boy building sand castles whether he needed a hand. Indignant, he refused, saying loud and clear, "No! I have two of my own." My father's hands tenderly tucked me into bed when I was the same age as that independent little fellow. Even when I was older, at five, after I had fallen asleep in the Volkswagen variant during many an outing that extended beyond my bed-time, dad would carry me out of the car and I would wake up but feign sleep so that he would lay me down on my pillow and as always, whisper a gentle endearment that meant 'my golden child'.

His hands on the joy stick flying transport planes for the Forces, had a world record for making the highest landing of that time. He was a handy man, nimble and quick with his fingers. He was a self-taught sculptor and his rosewood and sandalwood sculptures were so good that some refused to believe that they were made by an amateur. Sowed gardens, fixed, repaired, peeled, grated, cooked, squashed grapes and jamuns to make wines, plucked, played, taught, and much more than that; he was always a helping hand. The sleight of hand tricks he conjured up fascinated and enthralled. Even after Alzheimer's botoxed his brains, his body was active and even when he could no longer tend the garden or help around, his hands were never still. When mind and body could no longer do as he willed, he folded his hands in supplication. Those beautiful hands of my wonderful father had long turned to ash.

With a sigh, I returned to the room filled with laughter and banter. Sharvee had disappeared again. Raj mentioned that Sharvee's close friend had recently died of Leukaemia and that she was determined to keep his memory alive. He was only nineteen and had battled it for three long years. The minute Sharvee walked in, Raj tried to change the topic. She had a red diary in her hands. She went up to the Non-Resident Indian friend and said, "Uncle, you have to help me get this published."

Opening the book, he skimmed the pages and after a bit suggested, "How about we do a poetry reading here. There are eight of us and we get to pick the poems of our choice. I shall open with this:

TO

'I am not

The past forward

But the present

From a future...

Reach out

Before time

Pulls away.'

He passed the book to the person on his right

to the lady in a Pashmina silk saree with a paisley weave. While she scanned the pages, Raj urged the NRI friend to try the Bombil fry. The reader cleared her throat and began hesitantly,

Delivery man at the bus stop

'They stood

Bright, short, small, tall

Long stemmed, delicate, sturdy,

Differently shaped,

Asymmetrically symmetrical

Beautiful, in an oasis.

An arrangement, so radiant

In the morning sun,

Held carefully in work worn hands

Of the delivery man waiting

At a crowded bus stop.

They too will wilt

In more or less a day,

Quick to decay.

At the maternity home

How they glowed

Tenderly carrying little bundles

In pastel shades.

When they arrived
The welcome drink
Colostrum, hungry mouths
Greedily sucked out
Of tender moist nipples,
Of mothers, newly made
Health insurance's first premium paid.

Long, deep, short shallow breath
Between the start and finish line
Inhale, exhale,
In and out
Fresh, recycled, stale…

At the cemetery,
Weeds over run by blossoms
There, bloomed a nursery.
Stealthily they creep up and steal
As an offering to their gods.'

She asked if she could do another and the rest of us cheered her on.

Ablution
'I trust myself
And, don't doubt you

Yet you doubt,

Undoubtedly you do...

Scrub the doubt off, you said,

It sticks hard in your head,

Though I have cleaned up

After we have slept

In the same bed.'

Raj quickly rose from his chair and retrieved the red book from the lady. Sharvee snatched it from him and turning to her father's business partner, cajoled him into reading a poem she chose. Being a builder, his eyes lit up when he read the title 'Property Rights'.

He plunged straight into the poem without further ado, in a thick Punjabi accent which is usually difficult to imitate. Remember the movie "The Party" where inimitable Peter Sellers tries to do the Punjabi accent but is as unauthentic as Chinese or Italian food in India.

Property Rights

'A quick step,

A cross between

A jig and a fox-trot,

With unsavoury haste

So, they can deliberate.

They take their places,
We watch them, from
Plastic chairs set low
On firm ground below.
The moderator sits between panellists
Modestly, moderately
Left, right, off centre.
Like a charioteer,
The whip is cracked
And the moderator
Opens the floor.
A false start
The poise of the poet
Momentarily falls apart,
Verse in Caesura?

Do they articulate sounds in their heads,
Before they amplify thoughts
Through a microphone?

The harsh light, they say
Blinds their eyes,
Their backs to the barbed wire fence,
They defend their hypothesis,
Assonance, dissonance

Somewhere in consonance.
A learned imprint
Each tries to press
So facile
Lost in vacuity.
Brittle intellect, bubble wrapped
In the egoistic, somewhat toxic
Kind of plastic
Marked fragile, handle with care,
To complicate what is simple…
 Idiocy masquerading as intellectual.

The celebrated four
Seated on the dais
Stoke cerebral fires;
The tea vendor's sooty kettle
Briskly pours into
Miniature throw away cups
Three quarters full
Brown liquid with dregs
All that passes on that hallowed ground.

A sacred space raised in concrete
Glows in eerie incandescence,
An owl,

Scattered stars, so discreet

Look askance.'

"What was that? I never followed anything. No built-up area or carpet area or FSI! What property, yaar!" exclaimed Mr Builder as he waved the diary in the air.

Sharvee squealed, "Uncle ji, time you learnt some poetry..." He knocked the book gently on her head and giving a low bow, went to refill his glass. He swung around suddenly, began loudly,

"Ajeeb Dastan,

Jab woh thi toh mein nahi,

Ab who nahi toh mein sahi,

Arrey! Ghabrao nahi,

Yeh hain galath faimee

Ki mein hun pagli,

Mano ya na mano,

Janam janam ka rishta hain

Pehchano to jano

Yeh rishvat hain.

Utho meri sakhi

Hume apna ghar badana hain

Saath saath nibbana hain

Zindagi aur mrithyu

Jeene ka ek bahana hain!." *

"Wah! Kya baat hai!" exclaimed the lady in the paisley sari and she clapped loudly. *"Par rishta aur rishvat?"* The builder said, "That is the foundation of any relationship. Give and take is bribery. *Lena, dena toh rishvat hi hain, oh bhabhi ji."*

Sharvee scowled. Shovana, Sharvee's mum, got up to head for the kitchen. Sharvee stopped her and giving her the diary said, "Aiyee, you have to read one out, too." So, Shovana, stood where she was and going through the index, seemed to know which one she wanted to read.

Melpomene

'The womb

That grew the seed

You sowed

Was mine.

That red stain

Spread all over the sheet

Grew livider.

The tiny foetus

I willed,

You killed.

You watched her die

A breath snuffed out before
It took its first gasp.

She was our life,
And while you live
My love is dead.
I wish you a slow, long life
Filled with cold pain and searing regret.'

"Melpomene, is the muse of tragedy," Shovana said. She thrust the diary into Sharvee's hand and hurried out of the hall. Raj asked Sharvee to go help her mother. Quickly and nimbly, she side-stepped and started reciting without looking at the diary in her hands.

Primary Colours

'Like a can of worms
Let loose on my palm
They bite into my flesh

On the mound of Venus
A blue vein engorged
Straining to burst into vermillion red

I snatch my yellow hand

From the palmist's slimy clutch
Turning it over
Rub hard to erase
The forged imprint
Of a life lengthened by
Good health and phenomenal luck.

The future I know
Sucked into black holes
Punctured on my thinned skin
When the ashes
Muddy waters, so wholly,
Let your memory remain
Pristine and crystal clear,
And this
I bequeath to you,
Dear Cacamander.'

Sharvee's eyes filled up and she dashed out. A hush fell over the room. The business partner blustered, "*Yeh* cacamander? What it is?"

Raj smiling wistfully, said, "Friend *yaar,* in some long-lost vocabulary of old English, I was told."

He told the NRI friend that he was willing to pay for publishing costs as long as it was a popular, well established and respectable publishing firm.

Raj lit up a cigarette, and pulling out a newspaper cutting said, "This is what the dead boy's twelve-year-old brother wrote for the Poetry Page in one of the many papers I subscribe to." Taking a puff, Raj began reading:

Survivor

'We were four

Now we are three.

My parents bear

The loss stoically.

When the pall of night

Covers them from my sight

Do their tired, pained red eyes

Ooze tears into their pillows?

Do their choked voices

Silently ask the Lord

Why was that son taken

Instead of me?

Sharvee walked in. She went up to her father and asked him softly, "What time should dinner be served?"

(Translation of drunk builder's poem)
Ajeeb dastan – Strange story
Jab who thi toh mein nahi – when she was there, I was not
Ab who nahi toh mein sahi - now she is not, but at least, me…
Arey! Ghabrao nahi - Hey, don't fear
Yeh hain galath faimee - It is a mistaken notion
Ki main hun pagli - that I am mad
Mano ya na mano - whether you accept or not
Janam janam ka rishta hain - A relationship that goes back through birth and rebirth
Pehechano tho jano - If you recognize, you will know
Yeh rishvat hain - It is a bribe
Utho meri Sakhi - Rise my friend
Humme apna ghar badana hain - We must enhance our home
Saath saath nibbana hain - We must stick together
Zindagi aur mrityu - Life and death
Jeene ka ek bahana hain - Are just an excuse for living.

* * *

6

The Flaws of Attraction

Are there laws of destiny? Does life play out in parts that sum up the whole?

She dealt well with the nitty gritty when directed outside the realms of fantasy. The plaintive cry of reality cut through the fuzz. In sync was the ring of her cell phone. An unidentified number flashed on the screen. She took the call.

A metallic timber voice pleasantly asked, "Hi, do you want to proposition me?" In that stranger's tone lurked a smile. Her basic instinct was to slam the caller but curiosity raised its nascent head.

Deciding to play along she said, "Since this call I did not make, solicit I shall certainly not."

He let out a low whistle, "Phew! Not so dumb. Are you looking for adventure and excitement?" Pat came her reply, "What's on offer?"

"Oh, nothing yet…" he answered but was cut short.

In a dead pan voice, she retorted, "On imponderables I waste no time."

He quickly cut to the chase and introduced himself as a single man in his forties. He had a day earlier stepped into 'Book Stalk', a popular store. A voice floating from above had captivated him. Like Hamlyn's rat to the tune of the pied piper's flute, he scurried up a short flight of stairs. At the children's nook, on a large colourful rug on the floor sat in padmasan, a petite, light brown skinned, bespectacled girl- woman with a clear complexion in denim dungarees and a blush pink collared t-shirt. Around her in a perfect circle sat small children in rapt attention as she read from a large hard-cover book that had been rebound in a Tweety bird yellow with robin red binding. A thick long swish of a pony tail was half way down her slender back.

The fleeting glimpse he got of her was immensely pleasing to the eye. She may have been in her thirties but he could not hazard a guess. Not wanting to intrude, he quietly retraced his step back to the ground floor's magazine section. Picking up a couple of current issues, he sauntered over to the teller's desk. The girl, intent on her task, looked up briefly to answer his seemingly casual query about the story reading sessions. The Store Manager was the man to meet. The Manager informed him that it was the last session for the season. In a pico second, he glibly told him that his niece was in the well-known play school, 'Pink Tower' where parents were roped in to organize activities and events in the school. Could he have the contact details of the story teller to give his sister? He tried to hide his glee as he slipped the chit with relevant details from the manager's hand into his shirt pocket. As he walked to his car, he pulled out the scrap of paper and studied the name. No surname suffixed made it difficult to assume anything. He calculated that time would fill in the blanks.

Her voice was smooth and lilting with clear diction, and did he imagine something sultry in that pleasant tone? Perhaps a good singer. Suddenly he felt like Atlas. The burden of a long and lonesome wait had shifted. He made that first call, and when she ended their maiden chat he wished he had asked her more.

She felt a bit light headed after that call encounter. He had seemed pleasant and forthright. She was unsure of the needle on the compass. For someone who had never done a thing like that before, it surprised him that he was up to something so uncharacteristic. He waited many days for a return call. None forthcoming, he called her up again. It rang monotonously. After a long half minute, he cut the call.

A couple of days later there was a text message that read, "Hi, saw your missed call much later."

It seemed like a cue to try his luck again. She took his call this time. They exchanged pleasantries and made small talk. Long after the call ended, a surge of dopamine-induced feel-good lingered. Soon it became a daily ritual of exchanging news and views.

In their passage of discovery, she learnt he was the product of a North Canara Christian mother and a pahadi father from Almora in Uttarakhand.

When he heard her say that she did not really know what she was, he thought she was trying the existential route or being coy. She laughed away his disquiet by elaborating that she had been adopted from a Catholic orphanage when she was a two-month-old, though her adopted mother had been with her for daylight hours every day from the time she was a week old. The adoption formalities were finalised only when she was nine weeks. Her parents who had hit their thirties by then had waited seven years for a child. They made her the centre of their universe.

Her mum was an almost white, red haired, lightly freckled, bespectacled Anglo-Indian of average height from Bangalore. Her dad was a tall, dark, light eyed French speaking Tamilian from Pondicherry. She was raised Roman Catholic in an affluent family with a cosy home done up by her house-proud mum. Childhood had been snug, adolescence relatively carefree. They led her gently with a firm touch to the threshold of adulthood.

For a post-graduation in Psychology, she had chosen Madras. Living in a hostel made her appreciate home more. A well-adjusted and placid person, she was more than content with her lot.

She liked to think that she was the blessed child of a greater god. What she could not inherit, she won in the imitation game. A henna-Arabica coffee and beetroot hair mask fortnightly had turned her brown hair auburn. It was in shades of her mother's hair. Often spectacles were switched for hazel coloured contact lens. In the mirror, she found her parents reflected back – a perfect combination of their flesh and blood.

One day, on their way back from Serenity Beach her parents met with a car accident and were killed on the spot. Like many who attributed their lot to destiny, she thought hers had been etched in double lines. Having specialised in child behaviour, she freelanced as a counsellor at a couple of local schools.

The man on the other side told her he was a commerce graduate who worked in the tea gardens of Assam. He quit when he inherited his father's dealership business. Five years after he expanded, a good offer came his way. Having sold it for a considerable profit, he invested in real estate. He enjoyed the perks of being some kind of urban zamindar. He was also the sleeping partner in a tea export business and co-owned the tiny tea house that was run by the partner's socialite wife. The last week of every month was spent at a little cottage he owned on a half-acre plot that was a ninety-minute run from his apartment building.

Zee-End was the name given to that property,

and he had an interesting herb garden and a few fruit trees, as well as beds of seasonal flowering plants. The harvest of fruits and herbs were sent to the nuns at the local convent. He then bought back the herb breads and biscuits as well as jams and squashes at subsidised rates for Tea Cheers, their tea-house. His palm-fringed condominium, sheltered from the city's pandemonium, was barely a ten-minute walk from the heart of the arts and arty area that housed the boutique teahouse.

They both found their daily communion therapeutic. Somewhere in the beginning he had called up on a Sunday but she had not taken the call. Explanations were neither sought nor given. On Google she had checked him out but drew a blank in images, much to her disappointment. She had absolutely no recollection of him at the Book Stalk.

So far, he was just a voice. After a few weeks of tele-communication, he mustered the courage to ask her out. Very hesitantly, he popped the question, "Would you like to meet up?" Readily she agreed. They arranged to meet at one of his clubs conveniently located in her part of the town.

She dressed carefully in a floral georgette mid-calf length skirt in shades of aqua-turquoise, topped with a sleeveless white voile with delicate handmade Belgian lace accents. In her ears she wore her maternal grandmother's Victorian setting pearls. She never left home without her father's Omega watch, which was way too big for her slender wrist. So, it was worn high. Like a talisman it protected her in that steely clasp.

In her imagination he was a small wiry, bespectacled, bald, pleasant looking man. A middle-aged Dilton Doily, if Archie comic characters were allowed the efflux of time.

The man she met turned out to be tall, broad shouldered and slim. A dark French beard that did not conceal deep dimples and a well-seasoned head with poker straight hair, blacker than grey at the temples and with more flecks of salt than pepper over the crown. The rest of his head was black velvet. His blue-grey eyes had a hint of a slant that may have descended from the hills whilst he was very light skinned and had a gently aquiline nose. Her first glance of him made her pupils expand. She smiled shyly as he put out his hand to greet her. When she said, "Hi Daan, it is good to finally see you," he was charmed.

Turning the pale shade of a beetroot *raita*, Daan exclaimed, "Lia, at last we meet!" She liked the way he stretched it to "Leeeah". What registered with him was that she was prettier than the impression he carried. Her slender heart shaped face and honey brown doe eyes with thickly fringed curls of lashes framed by rimless glasses, evoked tenderness. Her nicely shaped nose reminded him of Elvis Presley's on his first album cover jacket. Her pale lips were generous and bow shaped. She had a wide warm smile. Her straight hair was long and thick, like the batter of a red velvet cake in free fall.

As Daan walked her to a table beneath a tamarind tree, he felt taller. They sat down and Daan gestured to a waiter. Before he could ask for the menu card, Lia quickly said she would like just a South Indian filter coffee, if possible. Daan ordered a pomegranate juice and chicken-mayo sandwiches. He looked sheepish when Lia told him she was a vegetarian. Daan asked the bearer to bring the menu card. Lia ordered a plate of macrons. They came in French chic on a pretty doily covered plate with a little glass dome cover. Lia was impressed. She insisted that Daan share the rose and guava flavoured Macrons with her.

As they sat in that pleasant precinct of Planters Club, a cool breeze fanned them, flowering plants in bloom, and the bright evening sky spread cheer even as Daan filled her in with details of the closure of his marriage. His marriage to a planter's sister had ended in less than nine years, almost a decade ago. His only child was nearly sixteen. He showed a picture of a tall, slim girl who bore a striking resemblance to him, despite her black cocker spaniel like locks that reached up to her shoulders.

Lia complimented her, "How pretty! What is her name?"

"Zimri", said Daan with a smile. She asked him what it meant.

"When we decided to start on the family

project, I had hoped for twin girls, whose names would be Zimri and Thumri. My mother was Zebela and my father was Tanush. Both names for my girls were related to music. Zimri in Hebrew means song and Thumri is in Awadh dialect, a kind of love ballad. When the baby arrived solo, Zimri it was.

Lia said, "Ah! Nice. I guess that is why you named your farm 'Zee-end'. He smiled in acknowledgement, surprised that she had quick recall of something he must have mentioned just once in passing. Like the unravelling of many a marriage, his too was messy. The ex-wife remarried as soon as the divorce came through and relocated to Phuket. Daan made a couple of short trips every year to meet his daughter there. On her annual holiday to her maternal grandparents, Zimri would spend a long weekend at her dad's.

Ruefully, Daan said, "I turned out to be just a part time dad. Missed out on so much." He looked away. Lia asked no questions as she could sense the lengthening shadows of past regrets. She revealed nothing of her personal life. They spoke of many things but the pertinent remained unsaid and unspoken.

As dusk gathered, she told him she had to leave. Much as he was tempted to ask her if he could buy her dinner, he refrained. Lia declined his offer to drop her home. So, he walked her to a cab. She thanked Daan and ignored the bleakish look he wore, smiled brightly at him as she rolled down the window and waved goodbye as the cab sped away.

Later, she sent him a text message. "Lovely meeting up. Thanks again."

Daan refrained from pouring out heart and soul into his reply. Wistfully, he thought that if ever he staged a musical for the nativity play, Lia would be his choice for Mary. She had an aura of chaste innocence. Lia had once told him that unlike many adopted children she never had any inclination to explore or discover her biological parents. Whatever drove a mother to give up her baby had to be extreme. Lia could not imagine her world with any other set of parents. She felt truly blest with a good mother, one way or another.

New calendars and updated diaries rolled in. They rarely met but their almost daily 'communion' never let up. Daan's sense of Lia was that of zen-like calm, sapient and good natured. Lia thought Daan was interesting and good company. He never wanted what they had to end. He was conscious of the boundaries but had found comfort that she had quietly become a significant part of his life. Could he reach out for more?

Daan knew that she was married and childless. He impulsively decided that their three-year-old association and tele-distance friendship had to be celebrated. They had rarely met up. He asked Lia out to dinner. It would be the first time they met after twilight. Lia had waited for this with an abstract yearning.

Almost like prom night, Lia wore a jet-black French chiffon sari with a thin matte silver border and a black crepe silk cut away choli that had badla work on the high back. She did up her long hair in a low chignon. A short string of fragrant jasmine buds was vertically placed along the length of the chignon. The 2 carat diamond solitaries that had been a 21st birthday gift from her parents, reserved for special occasions, were taken out of the locker and worn. Not a day went by when she never thought of her ma and abba. Like a mantra her mother would repeat that she was a prayer answered. In fact, her baptism name was Eliana, literally meaning a prayer answered. It was only after she lost them that Lia firmly believed that they were among the main miracles in her life. She wondered if she would have introduced Daan to them.

He had made reservations at Blue Bayou the only revolving restaurant the country could boast of. Lia stunned him. He had only seen her on those rare occasions in neat casuals and makeup-less. Her spectacle-less eyes were kohl lined and the coloured lens made them spectacular. Flawless, subtle make up and the lilac pink accentuated her lips well. How does one look sensuous yet chaste? Was this a houri with a halo? Daan asked himself. Cognitive dissonance in some measure swamped him. Refusing alcohol, Lia ordered a Virgin Mojito. Daan, a wine and beer bibber, ordered an Andy Erickson 2005 Leviathan Red. What the hell, this was a milestone being celebrated! Lia liked the way his dimples grew deeper when she asked if "wine, women and song" were his necessities and the order of preference. Daan looking her straight in the eye and said, "I am essentially monogamous and a social drinker, but doubt if I can live without music. Learning to play a new instrument was therapeutic when my marriage fell apart. Music became my salvation."

Lia let that pass. She asked for a baked rigatoni with broccoli, green olives, pine nuts and a mock pancetta. Daan ordered a spice roasted marmalade crusted roast duck. They shared flat breads with herbs and roasted tomatoes. A cocoa colonised dessert island was a chocoholic's haven. Daan opted for a Toblerone pudding while Lia chose a mocha affogato. It was an Amaretto liqueur espresso coffee poured onto a rich chocolate ice-cream topped with grated dark chocolate. They shared their desserts. When the curtain rung down, Daan asked Lia if he could drop her home and she agreed.

They drove back in contented silence with a piano duet playing in the background. Daan told her it was duet-andante with 5 variations of G-major. For Daan it was the shortest stretch he had ever done, though he did the five kilometre drive at an injured tortoise's pace.

When Lia indicated that they had reached her apartment building, he pulled up at her closed gate. The watchman ambled sleepily to open it for the car to enter but Lia turned to Daan and said, "I'd invite you in but Tzad is probably in bed." Daan turned red and said, "No sweat, next time perhaps."

Lia nimbly stepped out. She leaned over and, smiling contentedly thanked him warmly and bid him good night. He waited till he could see her enter her building foyer.

As if withheld from sleep, Daan was held captive to an endless wakeful night. The next morning decisively, Daan sent a text message, 'Lia you are a very special person. Can we take this to another level?'

When Lia opened the message, she stared at it as if a malignant tumour on a vital organ was on display. Though she had played out this scene in many ways over the last few months, ennui engulfed her. Despondently, she replied, 'Shall respond later and in person.' Daan, unsure of the tone, instinctively stalled. Like partners in time, they organized delay. Awkward, they both avoided each other. When Daan could no longer stretch procrastination, they set a date to meet at a coffee shop close to Lia's place. Casually clad in jeans, and an off-white smocked peasant style top that had on its yoke blue and yellow French knot roses, a high pony tail and with just a bit of gloss on her lips, Lia looked like a girl fresh out of college. As if colour co-ordinated, Daan was in a white polo t-shirt and Levis. After they settled down to cappuccinos and walnut brownies, Daan tried to recall a Maxwell couplet:

"Days are very many. Days are few

I want to be with someone and you are who."

Lia cut through his rumination. In a composed and straight forward manner, she began her story. At the start, she categorically said that her husband Tzad was a kind, extremely tolerant and good-humoured man who accepted her as she was. Baffled, Daan wondered why that was a moot point. The guy had all the luck when he got this girl.

Oblivious to his thought processes, Lia steadily continued that her husband, a Naval architect turned economist was generous to a fault. He was her best friend and had been told about Daan right from that crazy call to their daily communiqués, and so on. It was Tzad who had bought that string of jasmines for her hair on that dinner date with Daan. Daan listened in startled silence. Calmly, she told him that growing up, she had wondered if she had been the collateral damage of a rape. It had tormented her. Vehemently she burst out, "Why would such a conception be allowed to fester into human form? A birth with rights to parents, abandoned to safekeeping or worse. Whoever he was, who impregnated that woman, did he realize the depravation, the violation and irresponsibility of his act? What DNA links can I claim as my birth right?"

Suddenly, she tugged at her spectacles; naked eyed she looked away for a long while.

Daan felt his vocal chords had been knotted into an organic bow- tie, strangulating him. Turning back to face Daan, Lia put on her glasses and told him without a flicker of expression that her marriage had not been consummated. Before the import of her words could register, Lia related how her in-laws had been close friends of her parents. Tzad and his younger brother Amon, much older than her, were always in and out of her house. Tzad was in boarding school in Kodaikanal. And one of her earliest memories was of him giving her a piggy back ride around the garden. Tzad would bring her presents every time he came on vacation, read stories out to her when she was in pre-school.

Both boys were very protective of her and probably thought of her as the kid sister they never had. Tzad, a bright and promising student headed West for higher studies.

When her parents died, Tzad's parents were there to handle it all, from funeral to memorial service and beyond. They had insisted that Lia move in with them and till she got back on her feet, they kept her safe. Eventually, they asked her if she had anyone in mind for marriage. She said she was open to the idea of marriage but had not looked for anyone yet. Finally, when the younger son Amon proposed to his girlfriend, the parents asked Lia if Tzad would suit her.

Lia asked them to find out from Tzad if that was what he wanted. When he readily agreed, Lia called him up and they spent hours on the phone for many days. Lia, convinced that Tzad was not under family pressure or a misplaced sense of obligation, agreed. Since he could not come down, they had a proxy engagement on the same day as Amon had his. Almost a year later, Tzad who had completed his international assignment, flew back just in time for the wedding. It was beautiful in its simplicity, followed by a small and elegant wedding reception. Every single detail had been taken care of by her in-laws. Lia had known the family forever and she said it felt so good to address them as amme & appan instead of aunty & uncle.

Tzad gave her a wide berth and time to adjust to the new equation. When they realized there was a problem, he was in the days that followed, a man morphed into Gabriel. He asked her if they should together seek medical intervention. She agreed. When there was no medical recourse, they went for counselling. Even after therapy, nothing changed for her. Tzad firmly rejected her tearful, apologetic stance and plea for an annulment. He gently told her that he would never desert her nor love her any less. His only advice was they keep their circumstance under wraps. His take was that if he had no problem about the partnership and marriage, it was nobody else's business.

Lia basking in his strength, devotion and steadfastness, resolved to be as generous and caring. She thought it was unfair to deny him what was his due and a natural need and told him that as long as he was discreet and respected their home and she did not have to meet, know or encounter any alliance, he was a free man.

Lia told Daan that he probably found it impossible to fathom a union predicated on such an anomaly. "I just got lucky breaks all my life. Amazing parents, this incredible husband, loving in-laws. Not once did they even drop a hint or allude to our childless status. What more can I ask for, Daan? My life got entwined with the right people at the right time. In its own mysterious way, we forged an imperfectly perfect marriage."

To break the heavy stillness in the air, Lia startled Daan further by throwing a gauntlet, "Do offspring inherit the sexual mannerisms of their parents? Do sons make love the way their father's do? Is there an infidelity gene? 'A variant Dopamine D4 receptor gene induces flawed fidelity,' Tzad says with a chuckle. Is my condition a genetic predisposition or configured in the climax of a brutal intercourse, were it indeed a rape?"

She continued in a softer tone. "Somewhere there is a theory that organisms can pass on characteristics acquired in their lifetime to their offspring. An online inheritance which is basically adaptive changes passed on. Perhaps, my biological mother became infertile or frigid after my birth. Maybe, every cell in my being balks at copulation and invasion of swamps of wriggly spermatozoa."

Somehow, chaste Lia made it sound like a slut screaming obscenity. Out of her words rose an image so grotesque than Daan, momentarily disoriented, could not relate to the who, why and what of this unexpected turnabout. Lost in a bubble of infinite space, he blanked out, and Lia seeing his glazed expression decided to wrap it up on a light note.

"If I did all the average wife stuff like learn to keep my man satisfied in bed, produce babies or better still, had the same appetite and sexual mores of an average male, would my life have been perfect?"

Daan tongue tied, could not articulate even helplessness. He felt his insides being wrung dry by a metal fist. He tried to make the right noises but barely managed to say, "We shall continue to be friends." With a Monalisaeque smile, Lia stood on her toes and reached out to hug him. Daan stooped awkwardly and patted her clumsily on the shoulder. She slipped on her court shoes and they said a quiet goodbye almost in unison as she got into a cab.

While she wistfully hoped this platonic plateau would turn into a green pasture, she instinctively knew it was the beginning of the end. The mezzanine floor between friendship and relationship was a head banging skid zone. Gradually, calls became a thing of the past, and occasional texts exchanged became rarer than the red moon. Reality, a sure-footed intruder, had stepped in.

Daan immersed himself in music. He found it easier to reinterpret fantasy. Lia missed him. Like a dark shroud, rationality smothered the temptation to reach out. Daan was a guest member in a couple of bands. One day, through the local daily, Lia learnt of a fund-raising concert for the girl child. Daan was performing. Since they were out of touch, Lia decided to go unannounced. The auditorium at Santa Maria College was packed. Lia was certain that they would not be spotted. A vantage view point enhanced the whole experience. Tzad encouraged her to go back stage but she declined. They left as soon as the show got over.

Late that night Daan sent her a SMS, "Thanks for being there. Hey! You never mentioned how distinguished looking Tzad is. Hard to find a man who is so good inside out." He ended it with a hats-off emoji.

The next morning Lia replied thanking him and asked for his e-mail id. They had never used that form of communique. Daan promptly sent it with a footnote saying he looked forward to her mail.

From: Lia Sugham
Sub: 3 Questions
Date: Nov 7th 2007
To: Daan Dhulia

Dear Daan,

Thank you for a wonderful evening. Music is magic. To be so musically inclined is a talent you have in good measure. Amazing Grace!

Congratulations!

1. Was there music before Adam & Eve?

2. I'd have to climb a ladder to hit the high notes. Methought you were a hero in the orchestra. Right?

3. How would you explain music to the uninitiated?

Warm Regards,
A fan

Daan replied.

From: Daan Dhulia
Sub: Afford the hear
Date: Nov 8th, 2007

Dear Lia,

Nice of you to grace the show. Nicer, if we had met up after the show. You looked lovely, as always.

No easy answers, but for what it is worth, here goes:

1. Faith is best unquestioned by disbelief and for those who believe, the Genesis is a sacred narrative. As an atheist who struggles alone in faithlessness, Adam and Eve are mythical. Having said that, I am sure music pre-dates the garden of Eden. Birdsong and windsong would have filled the air joyously. Running waters, bubbling brooks, whistling wind, the song of trees and rustling leaves make good vibrations. No proof required to back that up.

2. An orchestra has many heroes, both conspicuous and otherwise. In life behind every hero lurks the shadow of some kind of tragedy. Since you made a point that escaped me before, I suppose in music every player is

some kind of hero. Just playing any instrument is vaguely heroic, I guess!? A conductor has auditory vision. He turns his back to the audience; like a rodeo star, he steers a motley bunch of artists of different temperaments, a plethora of instruments into scales of harmony, organizational skills, patience and the gift of fine tuning empowers him to make things happen. Another very conspicuous hero is the oboe, sitting right in front of the clarinets to the left of the flutes. For instance, listen to Marcello's Oboe Concerto in D minor. Simple but amazing. However, the worst job in an orchestra must be that of the triangle payer. And such small parts too, to suffer through so much rehearsal. In classical music, tension eases into resolution but for the poor triangle player, God help you if you miss your entry. After all that screaming in the rehearsal, it always seems so conspicuous exposed and all by yourself besides the temps. Perhaps, better to be an inconspicuous hero after all.

3. I cannot imagine a world without music. Its creation is compelling.

Like a heartbeat and breath, the spirit of music is a prelude.

By the way, none of what I write here or try to convey is original. My mother was a good singer who loved to sing the livelong day and probably did sing a lot when I was in the womb. I'd like to think my interest in music began there. Joining mum's church choir was uplifting. The choir master ranted about shoddily played music being worse than the sound of gun shots, and he believed a musician with talent but neither practice nor dedication was like a rattle snake in heat. That kind of whiplash was probably why I never remained a church goer. But I digress…In some W. Classical pieces, the musician needs to understand and bury himself in music more than lend it his own emotion. Thus Jascha Heifetz, violinist sublime would play with a seeming lack of emotion. Isaac Stern in contrast, oozed it. The truth of music lies in the purity of some choirs. Music became more right brained activity when it wafted into the artistic sphere. Music soothes, stimulates, even irritates. Take Jazz, for example. If it hadn't got that swing, it's all bling, in my opinion. But it is such fun to improvise; music liberalization!

Somewhere I read that playing a musical instrument is akin to aural pornography and singing is auditory masturbation. My Puritan mum would have had a seizure after proclaiming it blasphemy! Music is an undercurrent to our collective subconscious. Have you ever come across a national anthem that has not been set to music?

In very poor communities, socio-economic experiments have used music to elevate, educate, and accommodate the poorest of poor into mainstream academia or cultural or livelihood platforms. In our country, music blares out publicly, be it festival or wedding or funeral. Essentially, music tapes into a mode of communication that totally bypasses our language processing area. There exerts a Zen like state of Satori during a series of aha moments where life is a flow. Bach or Beethoven, music of the sphere, chants, hymns, emotion driven, cold play, catharsis, whatever. It is too much tedium to speak or write about. Like sex, music is best experienced.

Forever hopeful,
Your pal always,
DD

* * *

7

Karma Sutra

The October heat simmered. Candles and votives flickered in and out of sight, as an effigy of Ravana burned to the ground.

Ninu's cell phone lit up and a familiar image appeared on the screen. She took the call. Without preamble, the voice on the other side said, "Listen, reliable sources are abuzz that your husband is not going to get the post. His 'own' have hatched several plans and plots to keep him away. Warn him."

Ninu's heart sank. Putting on her 'to hell with the rest' tone, she snapped, "Who cares! What can we do anyway? If it is true that they have joined forces to forestall Chirag's promotion, we are no match for them. We've never been hit by the Godfather Syndrome!"

There was silence for a second. After a moment she heard him clear his throat and rasp, "www.Com"

"What?" she yelled back irritated.

"Yes, warlord, wealth hoarding and whoring is the name of the domain," his voice trailed off.

Feeling queasy, Ninu looked blankly at her phone. She was in a state of shock. How could one among them, someone who claimed to be their friend, do this? Now she would fight back. Closing her eyes and folding her hands into a united fist, she began to pray, "May the Sacred Heart of Jesus be praised, adored, glorified and loved today and everyday throughout the world, now and forever. Amen! St. Jude worker of miracles, pray for us. Holy St. Clare, pray for us." She felt her pulse rise and her throbbing head began to release the pain in waves.

The next day at the grotto, she went to discuss the matter with Mother Mary. It was not a dialogue, but Ninu had faith that their case would be given due consideration. She chanted three Hail Mary's and left with a song in her heart. As she was leaving she bumped into Mr. Patar, a former neighbour who had retired a few years ago.

"Is Chirag all set for the top post?" the older man asked with a snicker. Feigning a bright smile, Ninu cheekily replied, "There is time still, and well there's many a slip between the cup and the lip." Waving her hand and smiling genuinely she walked away, as Mr Patar gazed after her for a moment before shuffling away. He had watched, planned and plotted his career all along, but his big dream of reaching the top had crashed when he got embroiled in a legal issue. That was where he lost the race.

A text message came to Ninu from her messenger. *'Everybody says there are five in the fray for that golden chair.'* 'Good luck to the *famous five,'* Ninu typed back. As she walked on, Ninu began the Holy Spirit prayer. It was a three-day Novena; it proved very useful, very powerful and had always got her through. She had prayed for many of her friends. Not so long ago, a Hindu friend and a Sunni Muslim classmate were frantically trying to get husbands for their daughters. Ninu prayed for the Hindu friend first. She told her friend that the prayer would definitely work, but would take six months or longer. In less than six weeks Ninu was informed by a jubilant mother that her daughter had found her Mr Right. A destination wedding was in the pipeline and she didn't know whether to thank her friend or her God. Ninu immediately began the Novena for her Muslim friend. Two months later she got to know that an engagement had taken place, and the *nikaah* would follow soon. Ninu's daughter in a faraway land heard of these glad tidings. The next time she called, she asked her mother to pray for her best friend there. Ninu did, and it was answered shortly after. As a thanksgiving offering she published the prayer in The Tamil, a local newspaper since she could not afford to publish it in the national newspapers. The Tamil got the prayer printed in English without charging extra.

In fact, the first time Ninu had come across the prayer it was in a leading national newspaper and the beneficiary's name was T. Seetharamakrishnan. It was printed under the title **Thanksgiving Prayer** and it read:

"Holy Spirit, you who give me the power to see everything and show me the way to reach my ideal, you who gives me the divine gift to forgive and forget what is done to me; I, in this short dialogue want to thank you for everything and confirm once more that I never want to be separated from you no matter how great the material desires may be. I wish to be with you and my loved ones in your perpetual glory. Submitting to God's sacred will I beseech thee (Mention petition). In the name of the Father, Son and the Holy Spirit grant me my prayer. Amen." T. Seetharamakrishnan

It felt like déjà vu, a piece of history repeating itself. When Chirag's brother in another cadre was due to step in as chief, the reigning chief who was set to retire, became an asana bhakt. He rigorously practised Namasakarasana, Padangusthasana, Chaturanga and Dandasana in the long corridors. (Folded hands posture, toe touching and muscle flexing exercises were performed in many places). He tried hard with everything he had, to get an extension. Before anyone realized, a smear campaign had begun.

News spread like wildfire that Anurag Das was not interested in the top post, that the present chief was indispensable, and no other officer could fill his boots.

But as it happened before, eventually the powers that are, played fair and square. Chirag got his promotion and the post. Throughout the term however, there was little relief as the media kept filling out column after column from time to time. Immediate overthrow, unceremonious exits, and succession battles were written about. Speculation posing as confidential leaks was gobbled up whole by common and company men alike. There were busybodies trying to probe and elicit information right from the time Chirag was due to get his last promotion that would elevate him to the hot seat. Repeats of the same situation took place each time the papers came out with some snippet of his life through a colourful lens. Only true friends and well wishers allowed them privacy and protection. Ninu also made news in a few national newspapers, but that was another story.

Divine intervention prevailed, and the tenure was completed. The Das family had a grand celebration bigger than any previous celebration ever. Ninu was especially pleased. Her Lord had led them to a rock higher than high. A few loyalists ensured the retired former Chief and his wife got a small celebration of their own at the Big Fish and Flounder Pub. The main host had brought along a long-retired heavyweight. He was a big man, literally and metaphorically, but a man of few words. If he were bald, which he was not, may have passed for Pu-Tai. In his time, he was known as Panditji. No scandal, slander or scam besmirched his name. The less generous called him asexual, but above all he was a super-efficient office machine.

He downed three large pegs of Royal Lochnagar in an hour. Ninu sat opposite the big man. At one moment, she caught him with a look of unmistakable lechery. Had the mojito kicked in badly?

Alarmed, Ninu looked at her glass. It was half full. She looked up again and saw the look had grown even more lecherous. Surreptitiously, she looked left and right of her. There was nobody. The others had gone out for a smoke. Squirming uncomfortably, Ninu looked over her shoulder. A gilt edged mirror stood proudly on the wall behind her.

A self-love, so lustful, was a love with a future, beyond karma and karmic.

* * *

8

Jack-in-the-pulpit

They were no longer on the brink of civility. Like the poet mocking the cultural Czars who attacked pornography, the self-appointed demagogue drunk on half a bottle of single malt, slurred in a voice devoid of intonation, "There's nothing more debauched than fallaciousness. A kind of wantonness runs amok, like the spread of Congress grass on a bed meant for pansies and phlox."

No one recognized the nuanced jumble as a hashed-up imitation of a renowned East European poet. No one cared. Each one there at that point was an avatar of a cabbage patch doll. Remo liked to call his one-and-a-half-acre plot, "the Land". It was a consortium of lawyers, activists and academicians who had picked up seventy five acres on the foothills. He had but a fraction of that chunk, but how he loved to boast about it. Polite first-time acquaintances were impressed by the seventy-five acres at the foothills.

This weekend getaway was a popular retreat for the owner and his guest list included many, from the suburbanite, downtown types to exurbanites. Every Friday Remo would make his pilgrimage to see Flora and Fauna. Flora, the bitch with a luxurious black coat was a cocker-spaniel. Fauna was a fat ewe. She had no lamb as the mate Remo had procured was roasted on a spit fire by the villagers when it strayed into their field and ate the fresh crop. He liked to crack that old chestnut about how a Welshman befriends a sheep. Remo had first heard it from his pal back in Law College whose firm Remo joined later. Memories of Sanat were good ones, filled with laughter, nostalgia and deep loss. How he missed him. Lung cancer had consumed Sanat at forty two, yet none of the nicotine addicts had learnt anything from that lost battle. Remo had tried giving it up but the withdrawal symptoms wore him out.

Seasons at cross-roads, like strangers who run into each other in the hustle and bustle of a crowd, rains ran into a departing summer. As they collided, a meltdown in the form of massive drops washed away the heat and dust. The parched earth freshly laundered, opened her vault of emerald, aventurine, jade, and peridot, bedecking herself in shades of green. Earth's fragrance filled the water-cooled air. If petrichor could be turned into a scent, what a breakthrough that would be!

Remo, the eldest of three sons born one after another in quick succession, had been raised for the first fifteen months as the little super wonder. It impaired him for the rest of his life. Vying for attention from a distracted, overworked and tired mother while her husband was posted in some non-family station, made Remo a die-hard attention seeker. A good gene pool had contributed to Remo's sparks of brilliance, artistic leanings, aquiline features and streaks of insanity.

One fine day, Remo stopped flaunting his connections with the Nobel Laureate poet. When hubris rose, a nemesis in the form of a Sociology professor, a page three socialite, came knocking. The lady was determined to make him the keynote speaker at the grand celebration of a long dead poet at her literary club. In a pit of quicksand, Remo threw up his hands and confessed that it was a cousin who was a blood relative of that greatly revered poet of Bengal. Ever since that narrow escape, Remo refused to acknowledge the fact that he was the second cousin of a prominent, present day world economist.

The Land was a retreat centre for many. The owner was a good-natured, hospitable, generous-to–a-fault and wacky host. All who took refuge there were needy, irrespective of their pedigree, wealth, social standing, skill or talent.

That day, gathered around a terrazzo platform under a bower of a Rangoon creeper known locally as Madhumalti was an assortment of friends. A bag of mixed nuts of different flavours-some hard, some soft and some in between. A filmmaker who strung together clichés with a Greek flavour, combined spectacular photography and mundane dialogues camouflaged in a wrapper of Philosophy. His cast was made up of professionals who dabbled in amateur theatre. Remo, trained at London in Mercantile Law, had three appearances in the short film. He played a lawyer in the movie. Reel and real life were balanced on an axis of action. The movie had won international acclaim and the film maker returned with a few awards. The guy hailed from a community with high business acumen. This acute sense of making profit out of an Art film had the film maker strike a proposition with anybody who had seen and appreciated the movie. He wanted them to adopt it if they could, and have a 'baby shower' kind of celebration for wider viewing. He was also eyeing big corporate houses to adopt his celluloid baby.

A college mate who had topped the University in History Honours was a third-generation Civil servant. Unable to change his family history, he rebelled against the patriarchal career choice by moonlighting as an author. He had a keen sense of fair play and was led by principles that were an anachronism in his profession. His colleagues, both senior and junior to him, thought he was a misfit in Service. But he was good at his work and had earned a lot of respect and good will. Since he did not hanker after lucrative posts, he was not regarded as a threat by the self-aggrandizing type of officers. The buzz was that he had no need to secure his present or future as his father had retired as a Governor of a highly developed state and the family house was a sprawling mansion in an upmarket locality in the country's capital.

Bir, the bureaucrat, often went on long sabbaticals to write books. Four had been published. Remo popped out of the pages in two novels. When Remo decided to marry Nipa, his live-in partner of the London days, Bir had made the arrangements. From the wedding registrar to the Chinese take-away brought in plastic bags and brown paper packets that served as wedding feast. When someone asked what was for dessert, Bir rushed out and brought back four party pack bricks of butterscotch ice-cream. Old Monk rum, sodas and Cocoa-Cola were served. All this set him back by a good bit of his monthly pay even though there were not more than thirty wedding guests. The wedding had taken place in the pre-5th Pay Commission days.

The Welsh Soprano on deputation to the Indian Centre of Performing Arts owed her life to Remo. He had rescued her from a seedy hospital bed. A liposuction surgery gone awry had required emergency intervention. Remo like a nightingale, rushed to rescue her from that hole-in-a-wall hospital, and zipped her off to the best speciality care hospital in the city. Tourists to the city often mistook that hospital for a five-star hotel. With the entire structure all lit-up at night, it was a sight to behold. Wendy Thomas, cured after a lot of critical care, followed Remo like a lamb. Ironically, that made him the black sheep in his family.

Remo's wife Nipa shrewdly played her cards well. She chose to be nonchalant and charmingly disdainful of the two. She had told her mother in law over the phone, "Do not despair; one of the thieves was saved, one was damned." Impressed, the old lady rewrote her last will and testament.

That day Nipa had defiantly brought a young man who never left her side as if he were her assigned body guard. He was well built, muscular, hunky, attractive and wore a deliberately disheveled look. Cho was a playwright and movie screenwriter. An avid listener with voyeuristic tendencies helped in his line of work. In tow was his childhood buddy who had suffered a nervous breakdown. He took shelter at the Sarasvati Academy and turned to art as therapy. By way of introduction, he would say, "Am Dax, a struggling artist who has learnt that art and wealth shall stay divorced."

A police officer had come with Bir, the babu. Prem, the cop had made news for all the wrong reasons. His saga was the stuff of a James Hadley chase, Erle Stanley Gardner and Harold Robins thriller. It had comic relief, pathos, bathos and all that goes into melodrama with many shades of grey. In the hoary tradition of 'man smart, woman smarter', his wife who was in the same service as Bir had gathered her forces and made a pulp fiction of him and his career. His IIT brain and mathematics talent coupled with six-pack abs on a six-foot frame had taken such repeated blows that lesser men would have cowered or cracked up. Prem had overcome every assault. Cho the playwright was turning that sordid-morbid story into a three-act play. Prem, driven by ambition, was aiming higher. He had grand plans of turning it into a block-buster movie with him in the lead role. The underworld would help him reach the skies. 'Amar Prem 2' was the working title of the proposed film.

Narcissism bound them all together. Remo loved a captive audience and the audience made allowances for his generosity and hospitality. In turn they enjoyed the perks of free boarding and lodging for the weekend. Guests ate their way through soon to be extinct quail, partridge, soft shell crabs and sweet water gigantic prawns. Strictly vegetarian Cho averted his eyes from the carnage. He took stock of a bullock cart, purposefully transformed from rural classic to urban chic, as a well-endowed bar. Farm hands and villagers who came as contingent labour were amused by the capers of their laiyer saab.

Cho, always intensely involved in anything he took up, could give an orientation on whisky. That the secret to a good quaff of whisky was to add a dash of water, he could make anyone believe. He could give you scientific theories about water and guaiacol compounds in whisky. There were three types of Scotch whisky made in Scotland: 1. Single malt scotch made of malt barley, 2. Single grain Scotch that was malt barley with rye or wheat, and 3. Blended scotch that was a mix of single malt scotch and single grain scotch. He knew his single malts and could go into the origins and processes of each. On an Irish linen serviette, with a capped Mont Blanc pen he sketched an imaginary outline of the map of Scotland to give his lesson on single malts, flavours, textures and ways to imbibe the king of spirits.

Remo, lover of poetry, could spout verses in Persian, Hindi, Bengali, Urdu and of course, knew the English and American poets well. His dream was to turn the Land to a hotspot of music and performance poetry. A replay of the epoch Woodstock Festival was his game-plan. Yasgur Redux would be the festival name. Yasgur was the farm that hosted Woodstock.

Nipa's brother was well connected and networked globally. He helped his little sister and Remo in many ways. Remo loved having international delegates over. 'Open House Summit' was what he called them. Bir and Prem were his resource centres. Bir called himself an FPF: favour processing factory. On most he days prefixed an additional F to highlight his plight of being used by everybody around him.

Bir had worked with international agencies in some of his postings and was associated with the Consular Corps. Remo exploited that connection blatantly. Like all Indians, hospitality always notched higher when there was a foreigner in their midst, especially a light skinned one. Remo's love for applause was compelling. Driven, he designed wood-fire apparatus and tandoor stoves, and scoured the tribal areas for unusual food combinations. At their festivals replete with the one-day market, he would pick up *'kalai'* metal ware crockery and cutlery. The table top was where drama and art were plated and consumed, and encores were demanded till his overstuffed guests then retired to the wings to digest.

Like the owner, everything on the land was larger than life, including an overgrowth of gourds, cucumbers, marrow, pumpkin and greens. They grew in abundance, and after the workers had taken their pick, the rest grew out of use. Even the farmhouse grew organically. Like lantana it spread about the ground haphazardly. His blue print of a Frank Lloyd Wright's hallmark building had been marooned. The local antique marketeers had grown richer after Remo built the house, while Nipa honed her haggling skills. A plethora of Persian carpets, Afghans, kilims, and fine dhurries dotted the stone floors.

A beautiful, chic and part oriental wife of the Maltese diplomat was in love with the idea of a post retirement farm house like the one Remo had designed. It was her maiden visit, and like a firefly she flitted around, lighting up like a star from some erotic sky.

Remo asked me to take her around the garden. As I did, I pointed out the stunted fruitless lemon trees some New Zealanders had planted. A picket fenced area with a manicured lawn was akin to shrinking aristocracy rubbing shoulders with the hoi-polloi. Climbers of echites, bougainvillea, allamanda and rambling rose. A riot of colour sprung from the crinium, amaryllis, zinnia and anthurium. Pots of Indian betel leaf, holy basil and lemon grass were part of the assortment. Curry leaves were conspicuous by their absence. Where Remo hailed from it was rarely used, as bay leaf was part of their cuisine.

Since he wore his atheism on his sleeve, even I was surprised to find a shrine and burning incense in the master bedroom when we did a tour of the house. On a small white marble platform was a big black idol of some Hindu deity. Meimi whipped out her phone to take pictures. She asked in her thick accent, "Which god is this?" I called out to Remo to identify. He came in sheepishly and blustered about how it was an heirloom from the great poet's family.

Meimi, an Army student in university, had been imprisoned for falling in love with a foreigner. The Maltese student Marc Muskat had also been thrown into jail for a day but released as he was not their citizen. A linguist, Marc spoke English like an Englishman. They seemed poles apart but it worked well for them. He often told his tempestuous wife to write in sand the bad things and slights she felt had been done to her, but the good done and felt, to be inscribed on marble, after an Arabic proverb. Meimi called him Chiu-Yan, which meant superman.

Fascinated by the interiors, Meimi stood still, admiring a Burma teak shelved library. Remo picked out a small tattered book which was an anthology of poems. From a poem titled 'Feather', he self-consciously read a verse aloud in his best imitation of a British accent.

"My Lord, the devil could handle a shovel

Just like the undertaker,

But I have no axe to grind,

Between the index finger and my thumb

The quill lies; sharp like an arrow.

I'll die with it."

I knew he'd made a mish-mash of the lines and turned "fly" to "die" for dramatic effect. That was the quintessential Remo! Meimi, from the same province as Confucius, knew it was time to make good her escape. She quickly asked where the washroom was. Remo impishly led her to a double door bookshelf and asked to open it. It opened out completely to a quaint bathroom with cast iron and fibre glass sinks, flanked by old copper water storage vessels. Banana and Bottle- brush trees grew out of them and exotic orchids were growing out of niches in the latticed wall on one side. Behind a stained-glass screen of water nymphets, lay a state of the art jacuzzi. The water closet was the latest in bathroom technology. It was set to the East of the room and had been encased within ivy clad walls on three sides and an oval marble tub of lotuses was placed three feet away in front of it. In a shallow sunken pool to the far right was a pair of testudines. A fabulous shower unit was to the left of the Jacuzzi. I was tempted to ask Remo if *Vaastu* principles had been followed in the making of this one of its kind bathroom, but refrained.

We went back to the party. Prem was doing a demo of *sattu* stuffed *litti* and *choka*, a roasted cumin powdered potato mash with a raw mustard oil drizzle. Remo had recently got vinyl records and a beautiful German handcrafted Player Trans rotor Max with an SME Tone Arm, an Ortofon moving coil system and Danish speakers driven by a pure Tube Amplifier. Pete Seeger's 'This is your land' was played like a theme song. For Remo, food was Art. Sanat, his law firm partner was his foodie buddy and they loved to experiment in their kitchen Lab.

I was married to a musician, the only born of a former Director General of Police. Once, during my first trimester a terrible bout of morning sickness made me rush home from work. There I caught my husband in bed with a woman I had never laid eyes on before. She was from one of those "Istan" countries. Probably very professional at what I interrupted. Mercifully, I suffered a miscarriage and had the guts to walk out of the marriage. My ex father-in-law, then serving as the State DGP, made a very generous out of court settlement that included a two-bedroom apartment in an art deco building overlooking the grey sea. The lawyer who handled my case was Sanat. Divorced and blissfully remarried, my new husband was my lawyer. I knew what lucky felt like those six years Sanat and I had together. Then cancer struck hard and, in the end, unable to see him suffer, I begged my God to release him. He promptly paid heed to my plea.

A loving husband now in the past tense was my present connect with Remo, the Land and the people on it that day. I had made a smoky beet reubens and a *baingan raita,* date and mango chutney, pandan leaf thimble cupcakes and a China grass tangerine pudding.

At these pound parties, *gyan bata-bati* was the icing on the cake. Remo was holding court. From his arsenal of anecdotal stories, a long volley was being fired. I had dreams to relive and memories to remember. I moved to the plant Sanat had brought in a ceramic pot to The Land on one trip. It had a club shaped green and purple spathe which an American missionary had given us. It was called "Jack-in-the-pulpit'. Since Jack-in-the-pulpit is a perennial, it can live some 100 years. Sanat had said, "Keep this in memory of me. It will outlive all of us. Our souls can live on this Jack turned Jill on the foothill. All of us hermaphrodites as soulmates in eternal happiness, and in the dead of the night we shall dream our transsexual dreams in the androgynous dark, along with Dylan Thomas."(How he loved to annotate his conversations with the poetry of Dylan).

Remo never forgot. He collected Sanat's ashes to sprinkle into a circle we had dug with our bare hands. In the centre of that circle he had the ceramic pot buried with the jack-in-the-pulpit rising above the covered earth. The holy circle was enshrined in an elevated black granite cladding. Specially crafted mother of pearl letters were embedded into a marble plaque that read "In memory of my best buddy Sant Aniya". The missing A was never found or replaced. Remo thought it was Sanat winning a landmark victory in the case of 'Sant versus Sin' as that is how he used to pronounce Remo's surname, Sen.

Prem quoted a sacred text, "One who plants one pipal, one neem, one ber, ten flowering plants or creepers, two pomegranate, two orange and five mango trees will never go to hell." Remo ribbed him, "That must be first thing you do when you are posted to the districts where you guys get huge gardens to go with your sprawling bungalows! You can plant here since you now live in pigeonhole apartments. The sarkar has no clue about proportions or perks. How is it some of your colleagues get their official quarters done up with wooden flooring, wall-paper and marble clad bathrooms with the latest fittings?" Prem's retort about privileged members of Remo's ancillary branch wanting palatial and exclusive accommodation with Italian marble and all the works, was overruled by the lawless Remo.

Someone sparked off a debate on digital versus analogue, analogue versus heuristic. It petered off in less than five minutes. Remo then excused himself. After a long while he returned beaming, with a couriered package that had come from a publishing firm. He announced that he was probably being wooed by that firm for his manuscript, which had been in cold storage for the last seven months.

We waited with bated breath for the unveiling of his package. It turned out to be a copy of a book that had received a good review by his book critic pal. He boasted that the critic had said one of the main characters in the book bore an uncanny resemblance to Remo. It was a novella written by a first timer, shrouded in mystery as it was written under a nom de plume. He admired the cover and silently reading the blurb suddenly exclaimed, "Brilliant!" His on and off British accent was a carry-over from the UK from where he had been deported for overstaying.

Suddenly overcome, I tried hard to handcuff hysterical laughter threatening to escape. That book in Remo's hands was mine. The pseudonym was Remo's full name in anagram and both my grandmother's names as first and middle names – Miri Aleya Emerson.

An extant weed was carried away by a gentle breeze.

✳ ✳ ✳

9

Look back, Look ahead

"Better than a love story is a laugh story. Give me a Wodehouse any day. When I read him, all is well with my world, even when it isn't. I mean really, they give Bob Dylan a Nobel Prize for literature! He probably tried to be a Guthrie and Seeger clone. Even his Nobel speech is supposed to be unoriginal. To be able to make the kind of understated, subtle, nuanced humour that Wodehouse specialized in, is sheer genius. Anybody can churn out pathos, magic realism, art of darkness, Kafkaesque oppressive writing and Shades of Grey kind of stuff. To be able to make a man feel good about his rotten world with a turn of phrase and create a situation of utter mirth in such a classy way, is classic brilliance and so difficult to write. Not even a posthumous nomination, is really sad and unseen in the background of what is considered fine literature..." said young Joe, quoting, unquoting.

Always an articulate, Alpha kind of teenager, the young man was full of fire and brimstone. Joe was in town on work. He had dropped in at his friend's place. They had been in college together during their graduation. His friend's mother remembered how this boy, then a twenty-year-old, had foretold the political suicide of a brilliant Keralite who had given his brains some rest when he let a below the belt organ pick a new helpmeet and mate. In contrast her husband, in his early fifties, had waxed eloquent about the bombshell bride that this politician had picked off the tree of life.

"Mum asked me if I would some day give an endowment to my university. Why would I give a rich, first world country University money, when my beloved Xerxes could do with my sweat of my brow offering?" said Joe's friend.

"Good for you Smat J!" Joe had said. An only child, the girl's mother had given the names of all her unborn daughters. The boys in class acronymised it to "SMAT J". Some of them had forgotten what her real name was.

The year before they got into degree level, the College Reviews and Survey of Colleges had put Xerxes right on top. So, a bunch of students, alumni from Marie Joy's School in Munnar, decided to give St. Tefen's at Delhi a miss. Instead, they applied for Xerxes at Bombay.

"Go West, young man," was advice they took to heart and set foot in the city of tinsel dreams.

Mathan, Joe and Phil took the flight from Cochin a day before the college interview. Mathan, gung ho, told his fellow travellers they could depend on him. He knew Bombay well. His sister had been living there since her marriage, two years ago. Reassured, Phil and Joe let anxiety go. When they landed, Mathan told the taxi driver to take them to SV Road. The other two who were in Bombay for the first time assumed he was taking them home to his sister's. The taxi entered a Swami Vivekananda Road, and Mathan briskly told him to stop at the McDonald's there. They alighted and looked around. Mathan asked Phil to pay the driver. He then proceeded to take the stairs up to the restaurant. They followed. Refuelled, they were raring to go check out Xerxes. It was a reconnaissance mission.

They got into another taxi. Mathan told the driver, "VT chalo." A long drive later, the metre ticking away, they found themselves in front of a magnificent sprawling structure, palatial, with a kind of British aura around it. This must be the Victoria Terminus Station, thought Phil. Was Mathan going to take them in a local now? Mathan directed the taxi driver to take them to McDonalds. At the spot, they got off. This time Mathan asked Joe to pay.

"Xerxes is just somewhere here," he said. Cheered by the close proximity, they asked Mathan to lead them there. Mathan, confidently turned left and they walked behind him. He took them past some wonderful old buildings, past the JJ School of Art. "This was where Kipling was born," announced Phil. He recited, "If you can dream, if you can think, risk one turn, if you can walk with crowds…" Joe cut him short, "That's what we seem to be doing. Hey Mathan, you said it was close to McDonald's. This does not seem close by my yardstick." Mathan seeing a flyover, said, "We have filled the minutes with calories loss. Let us head back to McDonalds." Like the beating of a retreat, the young boys marched on with their backpacks. Sweaty and thirsty, they retraced their steps to the fast-food joint. Iced cokes demolished, Joe took the lead and asked someone if Xerxes College was anywhere in the vicinity. By then Phil and Joe figured that Mathan's was a McDonald's lodestone trail. Maybe that is why he opted for Xerxes instead of Tefen's, they told him.

The next morning the three of them scrubbed clean, stood at the old oak gates of the principal's interview hall. Each of them was told individually that mere attendance was not the only expectation, attention to academics not the only pursuit. Participation in extra curriculars was mandatory. 'Ex nihilo nihil fit', Latin for 'nothing comes from nothing' was the college motto. It encouraged them to find their wings fast and reach the top of whatever they undertook. Just a few months of being Bombay boys, and they had "Fun here" emblazoned on their dorm walls.

Mathan, Joe, Phil, Abiud and Manu headed for Colaba one evening to take a break from the tyranny of the warden and monotony of the mess dinners. They goofed around the Gateway and stepped into the Taj to take a leak in the luxury of the men's room there. It was opposite 'The Golden Wagon Restaurant' so they called it the 'golden pee break'. Lusting after five-star food was a waste of time, so they made a quick exit in search of affordable sustenance. Mathan declared that he could only afford the McDonalds on the causeway, so they headed there. Refreshed after their happy meal, the five stepped out. Gunshots in the air made them jump out of their skin. Mathan and Joe were all agog to explore. Jumpy Manu caught them by their shirts and dragged them away, in the opposite direction towards Regal theatre.

"*Aiyyo*, must be a gang war!" exclaimed Mathan excitedly. Manu almost hysterically shrieked, "Don't be daft! Just run for your life." Phil agreed. They made a dash for the theatre. Phil had previously booked the tickets. They got there before the shutters were lowered by the management. Once they were comfortably ensconced in the darkened hall, they forgot the outside world. Lost in a Bollywood potboiler, cell phones off, they laughed at the inanity of Hindi movies. It was far removed from the top drawer stuff that Malayalam movies were made of.

Once the movie was over, they were quickly hustled out by the ushers. The five put on their phones and found missed calls from all and sundry. Mathan had seven calls from his Mum and the others too had as many if not more. The road was eerily bare. A deserted Colaba was hard to digest. Taxis had disappeared. A few kaali-peelis were whizzing by. Manu in panic shrieked," F@#$%&@ s#!* the gang wars must have got crazy. Let's scram!" They tried hailing a cab. One of them slowed down beside them and in a trice four of them squeezed into the back. Mathan ran like the wind and jumped into the front seat. The driver unceremoniously told them to get out.

Mathan turned to him and in broken Hindi stuttered, *"Sir ji, hum ko dar, thum ko dar, sab ko dar, bahut dar, poora dar.* Please *chalo.* Go please, go!" The driver asked brusquely, *"Kahan jao?"* The minute the boys in unison shouted "Hostel in Bombay Central" he told them to get off. Mathan with folded hands implored him with "Please *sar,* please." Frantically, they called up their roomies back in the hostel. One of them suggested that they go the nearest shelter.

"What the f@#$! What shelter are you talking about man?" Manu screeched. Joe took control and asked Manu to keep it low. He softly said, "Listen guys, what should we do? We don't know any place nearby and this driver is shit scared." Phil had a brainwave. "That girl in our class we call Smat J, stays somewhere close to the Government Secretariat. Her dad is some big shot. That should be a safe place."

"Phew!" said Mathan "That should do. What is the name of her building?"

"I don't know."

"Jaldi karo beta!" urged the poor distraught driver.

Mathan told him, "Secretariat go, chalo!" The driver did not know where that was. Abiud knew it was called Mantralaya or something like that. The driver put his foot on the accelerator and they were on their way. In the meantime, Phil called up Adita, Smat J's friend. She told them to stop at a building called Snehala, opposite the Mantralaya. He asked Adita, who spoke Marathi to give the driver directions. The Driver was Bihari. In Hindi she told him where to go. The driver took them straight there. Mathan pulled out some notes from his pocket, thrust it into driver's hand and jumped off the car.

The gates were bolted. The boys could see a security guard and Joe timidly said, "Please sir, open the gate.""Please *kholo,*" Mathan repeated. The guard asked them which flat they lived in. They truthfully told him that they had come to see their friend. He asked which floor. They did not know. One of them said "Smat J ka ghar!" Another frantically said, *"Eda mandan!* It's Ayesha. Ayesha ka father *ghar."* Guard asked for her father's name. So Mathan said, "Ayesha Dutt ka father ka ghar." Guard repeated, *"Saab ka naam?"* So Abiud quickly answered, "Mr Dutt!"

The guard opened the gate and let them in. Joe asked Phil to call up Adita and asked her to inform Smat J that they need a place to stay.

Also, to find out which flat it was, as the name board near the lifts had everything written in either Marathi or Hindi which would have taken them all night to read.

On the tenth floor, Ayesha's mum had barely put the phone receiver back in the cradle when the door bell rang. She opened the door to see five scared boys crowd the passage. She smiled and welcomed them in.

"What happened? Adita rang me up and said, you needed shelter. Has the warden shut you out?"

"Aunty, thank you so much!" said Phil, "We don't know but there seems to be trouble in Colaba. We can't get back to the hostel."

Anu Dutt excused herself and went to wake up her husband. He emerged from the bedroom sleepily. He saw the boys and lit up a cigarette. Saying hello to them, he put on the TV. The breaking news was that there were several places under attack. Mr Dutt saw his batchmate, ATS Chief Hans Kanade, wearing a bullet proof jacket getting into a Qualis with a bunch of cops. Dutt was on a year long sabbatical to complete a novel he was writing.

"Oh! I heard crackers bursting a short while ago. I thought it was the usual wedding sounds as this is the season," Anu said. Her husband grunted a reply, then told her to rustle up some dinner for the boys and to wake Ayesha up. She hurried to the kitchen first and pulled out a loaf of bread and seven eggs. Then she went to wake up Ayesha who thought she was dreaming when her mother urged her to wear something decent and come out to meet her classmates.

~ ~

"Aunty, this year November will make it our tenth anniversary. Among my best memories of Bombay is the time we spent here those three days. What a time it was. Good food, playing cards, having drinks with Uncle, discussing literature and politics with him. It was heaven on earth, even if stereophonic sounds of violence interrupted our laughter. We were exactly in the middle of terror. Your apartment back then was the centre point between the two hotels besieged. Fun and laughter in the time of five-star terror, like love in the time of cholera..." Joe trailed off. He was admiring the beauty of the garden and the bungalow that was now the official residence of the Dutts. Ayesha had, on social media, put up a nice post that read, 'Proud of all my Pa did, prouder of all that he never ever did to get to the top.' Joe had tremendous respect and affection for this deeply grounded family. When Joe and gang had gate-crashed that nasty November night, her father had been on a year's leave without pay to write that novel. The book made front page news in one of the leading papers. Ayesha was unlike any *Babu brat.* This was a girl who had walked all the way from Nariman Point to Bandra one early Sunday morning to spend the day with the gang. They passed the hat around to send her back home in a cab later that day.

"Ayesha is in touch with Abiud who is in Wakayama Prefecture. Phil is in Wharton. Where are Mathan and Manu? They just dropped off the radar." Anu said. She quietly reminisced of the time when as the boys were leaving her home after their three days stay, they had asked her if she would like to adopt them. She smiled at the memory of her shudders then, for the mothers of sons.

"Manu is doing his own thing somewhere. We lost touch. Mathan did law from CLS. His dad sent him to Columbia but he hooked it from there, ended up doing Music and Movement at Princeton. He met a half Mallu girl..."

Anu interrupted at that point and asked what the other half was. "Inuit," said Joe. "Wow! Interesting. What is her name?" asked Anu.

"Manna Ahnah. Mathan had taken a video of their first date. Then he had his wedding proposal recorded. A video shot of the first time he went to meet her parents; the betrothal ceremony was duly filmed too. Looks like our pal had looked ahead pretty well. To video a first date meant he had a plan, a vision. Good old Mathan made an absolute production of the wedding. It was scripted, directed, and produced by Mathan and Mathan alone. There was Mathan swinging from a rope centre stage, jumping off the stage, Mathan spouting verse, Mathan dancing, Mathan speaking, Mathan being his own toast master,

Mathan leaving the bride with the best man at Church to go to the side of the Altar and croon a song he had composed for his bride. Mathan video's playing on gigantic screens, his radiant bride being his ardent admirer. At one point we thought he would sign an autograph for her. I won't be surprised if she has tattooed his name on some intimate body part of her body."

Ayesha was in splits. Her mother asked if Mathan was still a McDonald's fan.

"Oh, he ended up working there as his old man cut the purse strings when he switched lanes and defected to Princeton from law in Columbia University. His wife is a vegan and has turned him into one too."

Ayesha burst out laughing, "Must be madly in love! Vegan Mathan, Mathan vegan; it's an oxymoron! How that guy could bluff! Remember how all of you played Bluff with mum? Mathan won every round in the first five minutes and you all hailed him the champ of champs. He only got caught when the cards fell out from under his backside when he got up for a coke and rum refill…"

"'Officially Vegan' - a culmination of Mathan's artistry. Aunty, god was not up in heaven above, but right beside us during that taxi ride. There were great times in store for us that fateful night. Even a slight miss and it would have been a very different story," said Joe, looking back.

"Wodehouse would have told you to to look

ahead," Anu said, half in jest. "God is all around, and you can be the grandmaster, Joey. Check mate!"

"Aw ma! Don't murder Wodehouse and Chess!," cried out Ayesha.

* * *

10

Tale of a tub

Once upon a time, in a kingdom almost in the middle of the world, a beauteous and virtuous queen reigned. It was her god-beholden duty to fill the world with beautiful people, a duty she undertook with immense fervour and passion. Year after year she gave birth, uncontrolled, unstoppable. The demi-gods came from all corners of the universe, from the skies and the bowels of the earth. Flying Uncle Charlie's kite, they came to procreate and multiply. All that was sown in her womb grew, and through her birth channel and a blackhole they entered the world. They had absorbed it all and so were black beauties like the fathers and queen mother.

Then one day a kinky father who loved to play with toys and games drew potions from the elements. He rubbed them onto and into the receptacle. It was a powerful potion that took the queen to summits, pinnacles and heights never conquered before. She started having multiple births, bringing out babies of different colours. One day when the experimental father took the red of the rose, the blue of the skies and the green of the grass, a white baby was born. Amazed, he tried his hand at different tricks and soon there were ruddy, brown, pale yellow, pink, beige, and many shades in between, rolling out of the baby factory.

This assortment of beautiful babies grew with time and when their Mother said, "Your time has come," the umbilical cord was cut. With their Mother's blessings they left the sanctum and went out into the world. From that epicentre radiated tribes and clans, men and women who instinctively went forth to procreate. They filled the empty spaces with different graces and soon there were many faces in different places. Some were born to lead, some were happy to be led. They crossed the seas, they climbed mountains, they walked the deserts, they played on plains, they waded on islands, they grazed in pastures, they danced in the valleys of shadow and light. Over hill and dale, they turned dark and pale.

If you look at the periodic table of these peoples of the world you will find bloody battles, wars and famines, pestilence and scourge, good times and bad times. Construction, destruction, constructs deconstructed; the old forever replacing the new. Some kingdoms grew and withered, while others united and became empires. The empires grew and colonised the weak yet rich. The wealth of the nations became bones of contention and they let lose the dogs of war. Havoc, warfare, and skulduggery tossed and turned the wheels of fortune, the rise and fall of civilisations. What man did unto man was a tale so savage, so brutal, that the animal world thanked their animistic powers for small mercies.

But all that is done is undone as the cycle of birth and death, the laws of life, move on…

One day in the new millennial, in the demi-paradise, there was frenzy and amazement that a white prince had fallen in love with a brown girl from another continent.

"What's bred in the bone will come out in the flesh!" shouted an angry white subject.

Another voice in scornful tone cried out, "A lowly actress of half breed! How can our isle become her stage?"

An admirer exclaimed, "Give love a chance! She is no air head. There is clarity, ability and a number of skill sets in the woman. A good track record of being there, doing that, instead of tea parties and lunch soirees. She may be the change we need."

Another retorted, "She may lead us all to this dance of destruction. We shall be pickled by the rub of love. What a betrayal! May Day! May Day! A prince shall be her slave!"

"Redemptive love!" the black preacher in the pulpit of the royal chapel preached, as the stunned Royalty reeled. The Gospel music filled the air, "When the storms of life are raging, stand by me..." From the echoes of Eton, came the rumble of "Flocci, nauci, nihili and pili."

Floccinaucinihilipilification, first recorded in the eighteenth century. A word longer than the letters of the alphabet, it means "at a small price". The many millions of pounds spent on the Gritish Isle for change in the world order. Small change for big change, is wine into water.

Against the envy of lesser minds and many tumultuous lands, this blessed union shall flash the united colours of the human race, love against infection and still the voice of prejudice.

Long live!

* * *

1 1

The Curse of Alz

"Yohan, I have to take my shots tomorrow. Will you go to the M.I. Room for me?" asked Ponnu. "Don't worry, it shall be done," Yohan called back cheerfully.

Sadat piped up. "Saale! One of these days both of you will get caught. How can you take jabs for him? It is not a college attendance proxy where you can just...."

"We won't get caught unless you rat on us saala," they both shot back in turns.

"Yeah! And you are one to talk; everytime the train halts you make us go check if everything is fine. If we don't you're shitting bricks thinking the bogie will detach from the train and derail."

"Poda maire!" resounded in their barracks.

The three men were best buddies, young cadets at the Flying Academy who got their wings early. Yohan missed the Best Cadet Award by two points, which was a regret he carried for as long as he could remember it.

Sadat was quick to marry and start a family, while the other two remained carefree bachelors. When Yohan was all set to take the plunge, he asked Ponnu to be his best man. Ponnu applied for leave and reached Bangalore three days before the wedding. Yohan had fixed a date for the best man to meet his bride. But they reached the bride's home late, and the irate bride refused to come out of her room. Her parents, embarrassed, made a lot of excuses to cover up the awkward situation as the bachelor boys left. What followed was an impromptu wild bachelor party at the only sleazy bar downtown, with Ponnu egging Yohan on to make the most of his very limited carefree days.

That was over forty-five years ago. Their lives were by and large successful and happy in many ways. But then time took its toll. Ponnu succumbed to cancer. Yohan grieved bitterly for his dear friend. Sadat's life meanwhile took a tragic turn when his eldest daughter died after child birth, leaving two young sons and an infant girl for him to raise.

Alzheimer's struck Yohan. He tried to live as usefully as he could for as long as he could, but slowly, one small bit at a time, he broke. The Alz monster stealthily crept into his very being and began to steal his memories, slowly pouring molten plaque that shrunk his brain. It mauled and twisted his personality out of shape, yet it could not wipe out the kind and generous core that made Yohan who he was. Always loving and thoughtful, he looked high and low for a present for his daughter Molay. In an ashtray he found a toothpick, asked her if it belonged to him. Bewildered, she answered with a stuttering "yes". With a flourish he announced, "This was mine and so, I give it to you." Locking and unlocking his faculties at whim, Alzheimer's held him captive. Sometimes in anguish and despair he cried out, the most heartbreaking cries ever heard. One day he begged his daughter, "Help me, Molay. Please take me to my mother! No one understands my problems. She will know what I want." How could she tell him that his mother had been dead for over twenty years?

Alzheimer's final blow was a machete that savagely chopped and viciously shred every vestige of Yohan's dignity. A good, kind and selfless man had turned in to a frame of skin covered with bones and filled with excruciating pain. When the end finally approached, as he drew his last breath, the muezzin's recital of the azaan filled the air. Bathed and dressed in brand new butter silk jubbah and mundu, they laid him out to rest. At peace, he looked like he had a smile on his face. As the priest recited the prayers, rays of the early morning sun embalmed Yohan from the star shaped skylight of his British-style bungalow. Gazing at his newfound radiance in that celestial light, a hush fell upon the room.

Yohan's young granddaughter, who had been his strongest pillar during his dying years, was asleep. As she slept she saw her grandfather rise from his bier. He stood at the threshold of her room, peered into the room, smiled his beautiful smile and said, "Thank you, my child. You will have a wonderful life."

The ashes were never collected. His last lucid wish was granted.

Molay grieved for all that she could not do for her father. It tormented her, taunting and haunting her every single night. She needed help. Then one night he came. Her father, dressed in pristine white, looking younger than the handsome bridegroom in his old wedding picture. He drew near her and gently said, "I know how you grieve for me. There is no need. Please believe me, I am well. It has been two months since I left. And you do not sleep. Rest assured, I am happy now."

A week later, the autopsy report showed that Molay had died that morning of a lethal overdose of Sodium Barbiturate.

✳ ✳ ✳

1 2

Grounded

At the cemetery, Kabir stood in grave solitude.

A traditional tenth wedding anniversary gift was aluminium or tin. Clutched tightly in his hand was a white satin pouch. Father, his super hero, lay in the ground below. They had laid him to rest within the earth's ample bosom. The sixteen-year-old bent his head low. He felt that savage blow that turned him from a beloved first born to a fatherless child. How much of his lifetime would it take to recover from the tabescent trauma of that death?

The evening sky was darkening to night. One man's dusk is another man's dawn. The ghost of a cow from under the ground rose before his tired eyes. In the land of the dead, he found the lost memory of a six-year-old boy in blue, reading aloud a verse from a poem in his Standard English Reader, a prescribed book for class 1:

"*If a cow can moo,*

can you too?

Milk, cream, cheese, butter and curd are not just for the wealthy,

Vegetables, nuts, fruits and trees make us happy and healthy,

The time is now

To take a bow,

Before the Holy cow."

His mother, waddling into the kitchen, had promised him a baby brother or sister. He would become a big brother in less than five weeks, he had boasted to his friends at school. Mother was always hungry as she had to eat for two now. His father would bring her whatever she desired. Kabir also got special treats separately as the food his mother had was to ready the baby for birth. That evening, she'd had the urge to eat beef pepper fry and Ceylon parathas. Father would have to now cycle a longer distance to buy the best cuts. His love tempered the meals he prepared for his family. Kabir had wanted to go too. His mother held him tight. He squirmed and tried to break free. Her grip grew firmer as he began to cry. His father coaxed him gently into submission and promised him a nice surprise. Through a wail of tears, he bid his father bye. Little Kabir knew that every time father went through that door and returned, a treat was in store.

That night of the waning moon his father was brought home through that very same door, in a body bag. The man-lynching mob of the cow-loving cult, in their frenzy of bovine passion, roaring like raging bulls, gored a loving family man to a bloody end.

Breaking through the dread of his past this mourner, neither boy nor yet man, bent over the grave in enduring grief and lay the satin pouch on one side. With his hands he wiped the surface of the grave, then with a clean, checked handkerchief polished the tombstone. On the engraved and dated surface, he placed a pair of baby booties from the pouch. His mother had crocheted them in white cotton for the unborn baby who died before birth that very day, ten years ago. They lay side by side, father and unlived child. The tombstone only mentioned the day they died.

Daniel Keg, his father's best friend, had calligraphed a frame with words as senseless as their deaths. It was planted in the ground at the foot of the grave:

When pett puja killed

Him who worshipped the cow

on his plate

The unborn and the slain

Rest in peace

* * *